CHANCE OF A LIFETIME
AND REALITY CHECK

A Random House book
Published by Penguin Random House Australia Pty Ltd
Level 3, 100 Pacific Highway, North Sydney NSW 2060
www.penguin.com.au

Penguin
Random House
Australia

Izzy Folau 1: Chance of a Lifetime first published by Random House Australia in 2015
Izzy Folau 2: Reality Check first published by Random House Australia in 2015
This edition first published by Random House Australia in 2016

Random House Books is part of the Penguin Random House group of companies whose
addresses can be found at global.penguinrandomhouse.com/offices.

National Library of Australia
Cataloguing-in-Publication entry

Creator: Harding, David, author
Title: Izzy Folau: bindup 1 / David Harding and Israel Folau; illustrated by James Fosdike
ISBN: 978 0 14378 092 2 (pbk)
Series: Izzy Folau; 1 & 2
Target Audience: For primary school age
Subjects: Folau, Israel – Juvenile fiction
        Rugby Union football players – Australia – Juvenile fiction
        Rugby football coaches – Australia – Juvenile fiction
        Rugby football – Coaching – Australia – Juvenile fiction
        Rugby Union football – Australia – Juvenile fiction
Other creators/contributors: Folau, Israel, author; Fosdike, James, illustrator
Dewey number: A823.4

Illustrations by James Fosdike
Front cover image of Israel Folau by Chris Hyde/Getty Images
Back cover image of Israel Folau by Matt King/Getty Images
Cover design by Christabella Designs
Internal design and typesetting by Midland Typesetters, Australia
Printed in Australia by Griffin Press, an accredited ISO AS/NZS 14001:2004
Environmental Management System printer

Penguin Random House Australia uses papers that are natural, renewable and
recyclable products and made from wood grown in sustainable forests. The logging and
manufacturing processes are expected to conform to the environmental regulations of the
country of origin.

IZZY FOLAU

CHANCE OF A LIFETIME

WRITTEN BY
DAVID HARDING

ILLUSTRATED BY
JAMES FOSDIKE

RANDOM HOUSE AUSTRALIA

DANIEL

BAM! The forwards slammed into the scrum machine. It creaked and rocked backwards as the eight boys in their deep-green rugby jerseys pushed against it with all their might.

'Whoa, whoa! Hold it!' Mr Richards shouted. The boys relaxed and stood up, watching as their coach lowered one of the

1

thick pads on the front of the scrum machine. Daniel watched him and waited.

The scrum machine wasn't really a machine so much as a huge bulk of metal arms that held soft padding at shoulder level. By pushing against it, the forwards were practising how to form a scrum with an opposing team, just like on game day.

To finish that afternoon's training session, Mr Richards had wanted the boys to practise getting the ball from the scrum to the distant wing as quickly as possible. Daniel, the team's captain and fly-half, knew exactly what he needed to do. If only the forwards would hurry up and get their act together.

'All right, one more time,' Mr Richards said.

The forwards put their arms around each other, bent down and slammed into the machine, panting and grunting. The scrum-half fed the ball to the scrum by throwing it into their collection of feet. The ball came out the back and he expertly passed it to Daniel. Daniel ran forward a few steps, imagining the opposition charging towards him, before shooting the ball to the inside centre. From there, the ball zipped all the way down the line of backs that were spread out across the field, ending up in the hands of the winger on the far side. He put the ball down over the tryline, signalling the end of another sweaty training session.

'Well done!' Mr Richards shouted, clapping his hands enthusiastically, then waved for his team to gather in front of him. Once the players sat on the ground, the coach continued. 'Great work today, boys. We're starting to remove those kinks in our back line. Remember to watch Daniel – he's the key. As soon as that ball is fed, you should be watching and ready, but don't move off your line early.'

'No, sir,' the boys replied.

'Right, well, the last game of the season will be our toughest – everyone knows that – but St Martin's are the only thing standing between us and an undefeated season, and I know we'll be ready on Saturday.'

'Green. And. WHITE! Green. And. WHITE!' the boys chanted in response.

'Now, before you go home, I have some good news and some bad news.' Mr Richards looked behind him and saw that most of the boys' parents were now waiting in the distance. 'The bad news isn't unexpected – Johnno still hasn't fully recovered from his tonsillitis, so William will be in the centre – no big deal, we'll be fine . . .'

Daniel sat in the grass, watching the late-winter sun slowly disappear behind a grey cloud. He shivered with excitement, anticipating what was coming next.

'But now for the good news,' Mr Richards announced.

Daniel looked up at his coach's face and their eyes met.

'Daniel, could you come up here, please?'

It's actually happening, Daniel thought, glancing over at his dad. He walked around his teammates' sprawled legs and stood next to Mr Richards. 'We all know about the rep team – how the selectors were here to watch us play. Well, this morning I received a telephone call advising me that our very own Daniel has been selected to play for the Valley rep team at the State Championships in a few weeks.'

The other boys cheered and clapped. Whoops echoed around the field. But, best of all, Daniel could hear his dad shouting congratulations from two hundred metres away.

Mr Richards smiled. 'I was also informed that the team will be going on a two-week tour before the Championships begin, and that the team will be coached by . . .'

Izzy Folau! Izzy Folau! Daniel repeated over

and over in his mind, wishing it might actually be his all-time favourite rugby player.

'Israel Folau!'

The team clapped and cheered again as Daniel's jaw hung open. 'What! Really?' he said. 'Are you serious, sir?'

'You bet!' Mr Richards shook Daniel's hand. 'You'll be getting your rep jersey at tomorrow's assembly. Congratulations, I'm sure you will do Barton Grammar proud.'

'Yes, sir,' Daniel answered before he was mobbed by his team. All the boys slapped him on the back and said how jealous they were of him. Daniel tried to soak it all up, but he was in shock to think that he was going to be coached by the greatest of the greats – Izzy Folau.

Soon enough, the cheers died down and one by one the others walked off the oval until Daniel was the only player left on the field. He looked up at the gigantic goalposts and tried to settle his thoughts.

This was a big deal. It wasn't just the fact that he was going on a trip with Izzy Folau. Daniel knew that being selected for the rep team was the first step to becoming a Wallaby himself. It was all he'd ever wanted. Now, just as his dad had predicted many times, his dreams were starting to come true.

Daniel picked up the football from near the touchline, along with his kicking tee. He decided to start with a hard one. He put the kicking tee at the corner of the touchline and the 22-yard line. He looked at the goalposts and exhaled slowly. It would be hard to get the distance let alone the angle, but he wanted to try. He thought back to just days before, when he'd watched Izzy being interviewed on TV after a loss.

'We tried our best,' Izzy had said. 'We didn't win, but we gave it our best shot and that's what matters most.'

Daniel sighed, remembering how his dad had grunted when he'd heard Izzy say that. He'd called it 'loser talk'. Daniel looked at the posts again. Whether he kicked the goal or not, he wanted to give it a go – just like Izzy – no matter what his dad thought about him.

He considered the ball and sniffed it. The smell of a rugby ball always made him smile. He flicked the ball into the air, making it spin briskly as it popped upwards before falling back into his hands. He flicked it again, watching as it seemed to hang in the air, almost magically.

A voice echoed across the empty grounds, shaking him from his thoughts. 'Daniel! It's goal-kicking practice, not time-wasting practice. Let's go!'

He turned to see his dad watching him, his phone pressed to his ear as always. Daniel nodded and put the ball on the tee before measuring his run-up. He stood at his spot, breathing deeply. He looked at the ball, then at the goalposts and back at the ball, imagining how best to kick it. He replayed the goal kick twenty times in his imagination before going for it. Finally, he jogged towards the

ball, balanced his body and let his foot force-fully yet gently connect with it.

It was a great goal.

His dad clapped on his knee from the stands, and Daniel smiled his biggest smile since Christmas as he ran after the ball. The rep team, the tour *and* Izzy Folau – it was almost too good to be true.

SIONE

Sione lay on his bed, holding his football. It was hardly white anymore. He thought back to when he'd first got it, before all the scratches and scuff marks, to his birthday over six months ago, and smiled. He'd been so excited, even though the gift wasn't a surprise at all. He remembered his aunt handing him the football-shaped present and laughing about how hard it had been to wrap. It hadn't mattered to Sione, though. He'd been so grateful for the ball that he'd actually hugged Aunty. And that was probably the first time he had ever hugged her – or anyone, really.

He flicked the ball above his head, watching it spin in the air for that split second as it hovered. It was almost like magic.

For the millionth time, Sione wished he could fly like a football. That way, he'd be able to go wherever he wanted, whenever he wanted. When things got tough, he could just rise above it and hide in the clouds for a while.

Sione kept throwing the ball into the air, remembering the first time he'd thrown it, and the squeal he had let out when it landed

in mud. The other Tigers had laughed at him then. They'd thought it was hilarious that Sione should treat his new ball like a newborn baby. But of course he would – it was special.

Now, each splat of mud or scratch from a football boot was like a badge of honour, a mark that told a story of an amazing try or a thumping tackle.

Lost in his daydream, Sione missed catching his ball and it bounced across his bedroom floor. He sighed and rolled over, his eyes coming to rest on the Izzy Folau poster taped to his wall. The Wallaby was smiling wide and running across ANZ Stadium, on his way to a match-winning try beneath the posts.

Sione had studied that poster so often that he'd invented names for all the tiny specks of faces that he could see in the crowd behind Izzy. He could smell the wet grass, he could feel a thumping in his chest. He wished he was on the Australian team, running alongside Izzy.

The phone in the kitchen rang, and Sione could hear his dad walking towards it. Those footsteps were unmistakable; the heavy work boots almost shaking the house as he walked, unlike his little sister's *slap-slap-slapping* across the floorboards, or his aunt's quiet padding.

Sione couldn't make out the words but it was a long conversation. That meant it wasn't a salesperson. It was probably a relative, or maybe even his mum. Sione closed his

17

eyes tight, trying to lift his body off the bed and into the clouds with the power of his mind.

'Sione!' his dad called.

Sione's eyes snapped open and he sat up.

'Sione! Get your butt out here!'

He stood up as his little sister's slapping footsteps approached at double speed.

Mele burst into the bedroom and tugged at her brother's rugby shorts. 'Sione's butt! Sione's butt!' she sang, pushing him into the hall.

'Okay, okay, I'm coming!' Sione followed Mele into the kitchen, where their dad stood, leaning on the counter, his back to them. His dad had the usual dirt marks all over his legs and was wearing his neon-green work shirt.

Sione wondered if each of the marks told a story like the ones on his football did.

His dad turned around, looking exhausted as usual. He stared at Sione without saying anything. Mele ran up to his dirty, hairy legs and he swung her up in one swift movement.

'Sione . . .'

Sione braced himself for what sounded like bad news. But the fact that his dad wasn't shouting meant he wasn't in trouble. *So what is it?* he thought to himself.

'That was Terry,' his dad continued. 'Sione . . .'

What's wrong? Why is it so hard for him to spit it out? Have I been kicked off the team?

'Son, you've been picked for the rep team.'

'The rep team?' Sione repeated.

'The Valley team. You've been selected to play for Valley at the State Championships!'

It took Sione a moment for his brain to register what he was hearing, and then he remembered. His coach, Terry, had put some names forward to the selection committee; selectors had even come to watch the Tigers train and play a game. But Sione hadn't given it another thought – he'd never dreamed he would be selected.

'Why me?' he said. 'I'm not even good enough to play for Valley.'

'Don't be so down on yourself, Si,' his dad said, lowering Mele to the ground. 'You're good.'

Those words echoed around the kitchen as if it were a cave. No matter how many times he heard them, he would never believe it.

'If I'm so good, why aren't you smiling?' Sione asked.

His dad sighed. 'Before the Championship weekend, the Valley team is going on a two-week tour. They'll train together, play other teams from around the country, do all this team-building stuff. Oh, and Izzy Folau will be their coach.'

'What?!'

'Each team in the state has been assigned a famous player to coach them, and apparently Valley got Izzy.'

This is amazing! By the end of the two weeks I'll be best friends with my favourite player of all time!

'Are you kidding me?' Sione said. 'That's awesome!'

His dad shook his head. 'It's true, but the thing is . . . most of what you need is covered – they give you the uniforms and the kit – but each player's family has to cover the cost of sending you on the trip around the country and, well . . .' Sione's dad leant against the kitchen counter. He didn't finish his sentence – he didn't need to.

Sione fought back tears, turning his eyes into brick walls that nothing could pass through. He was good at doing that – hiding his emotions. It was something he had done many times.

Why did Terry put my name down for this? he thought, clenching his fists and looking away from his dad.

An unexpected noise sounded as the front doorknob clicked and turned before Sione's aunt bustled in.

'You'll never guess what –' She stopped mid-stride as she stared at her brother and nephew standing silently in the kitchen. 'What's wrong?' she asked, placing a bag of groceries on the floor.

Sione looked up at her, his face burning.

'What is it, Sione?' she asked.

He screwed up his eyes, trying to respond without letting a tear fall. When he finally spoke, his voice was cracked and high-pitched.

'I got selected for the rugby rep team,' he said. With that, he walked down the hall, slammed his bedroom door and collapsed onto his bed.

DANIEL

Friday assemblies were usually the most boring thing on earth. The school hall was a large, cavernous room that became hot and stuffy when a thousand boys crammed in after lunch each week. Daniel and his friends always tried to sit in one of the back corners, out of sight from teachers, where they could whisper about their next rugby match. Today, Daniel sat right in the middle of the assembly hall, where the headmaster would be looking in his direction the whole time, but Daniel didn't care. This assembly was going to be sweet.

Once the hall was full, the school captain called for everyone to rise. The headmaster and deputy principal walked in, up the stage steps and stood facing the students, awaiting the national anthem.

Soon, I'll be up there too, Daniel thought.

He usually couldn't be bothered singing the anthem, but today he sang each word loud and clear. His friends on either side of him did the same. They all stood straight and tall, proud of Daniel and the fact that he – now destined for great things — was their friend. Knowing this made Daniel sing even louder.

His best friend, Steve, glanced over and laughed. 'What's up with you, Mr Opera Singer?'

Eventually, the headmaster announced the big news that Daniel Masters had made the rugby rep team. The entire crowd of students broke out into applause in a way Daniel had never heard. He couldn't help but grin as he walked down his row and out into the aisle, lapping up the attention.

Everyone was still clapping as he stepped onto the stage. Barton Grammar prided itself on rugby, and Daniel was now one of its stars. Mr Richards appeared from somewhere back-stage and was holding a roll of green material that Daniel assumed was his new rep jersey. *Green — just like Barton's colours*, he thought to himself.

It felt so foreign to be up there, but Daniel was loving every second of it. A thousand faces were looking at him. He could only just make out his empty chair in the middle of the hall.

Mr Richards leant in to the microphone. 'It gives me great pleasure to present Daniel with this jersey. I am proud of all he has accomplished this season; his representative selection is well deserved. I know that he will represent Valley — and Barton Grammar — as brilliantly as anyone can.'

He then shook Daniel's hand as Mr Varnes, the school photographer, snapped away.

The jersey unravelled, and Mr Richards and Daniel each held up one shoulder and sleeve of the precious garment as more photos were taken. Daniel didn't think his cheeks could handle much more smiling.

'And now,' the headmaster said to the school, 'I would like to read out an email that we received this morning from Israel Folau, the Valley team's coach.'

Excited whispers filled the hall.

'Congratulations, Daniel,' the headmaster read aloud, 'on your selection to the Valley team. I can't wait to meet you and start training together in preparation for the State Championships.' Daniel's chest puffed out and his hands grew clammy. 'Every time I have faced a new challenge, I have felt anxious and unsure, but also extremely excited. I hope you are pleased with your selection and are looking forward to all the fun we will have as a team. Izzy.'

The headmaster nodded at the school captain, who shouted, 'Three cheers for Daniel. Hip hip!'

'Hooray!' the school chorused.

'Hip hip!'

'Hooray!'

'Hip hip!'

'Hooray!'

Daniel threw his schoolbag onto the back seat of his father's car and jumped in.

'Congratulations!' his dad said, looking back at him from the driver's seat. 'It's really happening, huh?'

The car pulled out from the school's kiss-and-drop zone and Daniel put on his seatbelt, making sure not to crease his jersey.

'What happened at the assembly?'

'Not much,' Daniel answered. 'Everyone clapped and Mr Richards shook my hand.'

'Nice!'

'The headmaster read out a letter from Izzy.'

'Really?' his dad said. 'What did it say?'

Daniel shrugged. 'Just that we're going to have fun and stuff.'

'Hmm.'

'What?'

31

'I would have thought that a coach – of a *youth* rep team, especially – would be all about geeing up his players to be the best they can be on the field,' Daniel's father said. 'His job is to toughen you up and show you how to win at the highest level. You don't need to be shown how to have fun – winning *is* fun!'

Daniel had heard all of this before and knew it wasn't worth disagreeing, so he just said nothing.

The rest of the car ride was silent except for the couple of times his dad asked about the game against St Martin's the next day. Daniel had actually forgotten all about the match, as important as it was. Somehow, in the past twenty-four hours, tomorrow's game had gone from being the final and possibly record-breaking match of the season to a non-event. Now that he was on the rep team, how he performed seemed irrelevant. Daniel sighed. Maybe he would try doing what Izzy had talked about and just have some fun.

After picking Daniel up from school, Mr Masters always went back to work for a couple of hours. For Daniel, this usually meant homework time – but not on Fridays. On Fridays he was allowed to practise his goal kicking in the park.

Daniel got out of the car and ran to get changed into his training gear. He neatly folded the rep jersey and placed it on his pillow. He paused, thinking how that would have made his mum smile. Then he gathered up a ball, his house keys and a water bottle and was gone, jogging down the street to the only place he ever truly felt at home.

SIONE

'Izzy grabs the ball and runs hard, sidestepping one defender, pushing away another, and passes the ball just before he's taken out. It's a beautiful cut-out pass that skips the centre and lands in the hands of the winger. Izzy falls on the ground with his arms outstretched. It's a try!'

The other players picked up Izzy and brushed the dirt off him, cheering and hollering. Lunchtimes at Valley North Primary School were always the same. Fifteen to thirty boys would gather on the grass to play touch footy while teachers supervised, ensuring little kids weren't getting trampled. Lately, Sam, who had broken his leg, would commentate, hobbling along on his crutches, trying to keep up with the play. The other boys had said that the commentary had made their games feel more real, like on TV, and so they had started pretending they were Wallabies. The only problem was that everyone seemed to want to be Israel Folau.

'There's the tap to restart play,' Sam shouted from the middle of the field. 'Izzy takes it a few metres before passing the ball to Izzy. Izzy passes it to Izzy, down the back line it goes. They're trying to keep it from the opposition, who are coming in fast. And Izzy has kicked the ball, high and for touch. It does go out, but almost immediately. The team has only made about ten metres all up.'

Sione sighed and braced himself for his team's comments. He had kicked an absolute shocker. But no one said anything. He quickly got into position to wait for the line-out that would bring the ball back into play, as anxious thoughts swirled around in his mind. *How did the rep selectors get it so wrong? Why had they put him in this situation of being selected but unable to go?* Sione wished they'd never selected him in the first place.

The ball bounced clumsily over the hands and heads of ten or so Izzys, all scrambling to gain control of the ball, before it landed in the grip of one of the boys on Sione's team. The boys weren't allowed to play tackle, so as soon as that boy was touched by a defender he had to stop. He tapped the ball on his foot and passed it to Sione. He wasn't really expecting it and so didn't have time to think about what he would do next. Somehow, he slipped his body between two defending Izzys and was clear. He ran hard alongside the touchline for about twenty metres, until he was past the tryline. He put the ball down. The whole thing had seemed to take about two seconds.

Sione turned to see everyone looking at him with their eyes wide and their jaws hanging open. Sam had even stopped commentating. *What have I done now?* Sione thought.

'Um, how did you do that?' Sam asked.

Sione shrugged his shoulders. Strange things like that happened when he played for the Tigers, too, and Sione had no idea why or how.

'Those two guys were right in front of you,' Sam said. 'How did you get through them without even being touched?'

'I dunno,' Sione replied softly.

'That happened in our match last week, too,' Thomas, a Tigers player, said. 'Our coach calls Sione "Eel" because he can slip through the defence line like that. Before they even realise he's through, he's gone.'

The bell rang, signalling the end of lunch.

Sione breathed a sigh of relief, glad to have the attention off him.

The boys trudged up the hill from the back of the school, towards the concrete playground and the row of bubblers that looked so inviting after all their running around. But going as quickly as Sam could manage on his crutches meant that by the time they got to have a drink, Sione and his friends were the only students left in sight – everyone else was lining up outside their classrooms.

'Sione Taito!' Ms Collier, the deputy principal, boomed from across the deserted playground. 'I'd like to speak to you for a moment, please.'

The boys froze. They had been caught getting back to class late. Sione felt sick.

His dad wouldn't be happy when he learnt that Sione had got in trouble at school.

Ms Collier walked over to the group. 'The rest of you, hurry back to class and tell Sione's teacher he's with me.'

'Yes, Ms Collier,' the boys said, glancing back at Sione a couple of times to try to judge the level of strife he was in.

Sione stared at his feet. The deputy was tall and imposing, like the Year 12 rugby players who pushed past him at the train station and who stormed onto the training field before his team had finished every Tuesday night.

'You're not in trouble,' Ms Collier said, but Sione still didn't look up. The gritty asphalt below his feet went blurry. 'Congratulations on your rugby selection,' she added, before handing him a white piece of paper folded neatly in half. He reached for it slowly but didn't open it.

'It's an email from Israel Folau, just for you,' she said. 'Read it – I think you'll like it.'

Sione smiled, but stopped when he saw Ms Collier watching him. He couldn't wait for this conversation to be finished so he could read the email in private.

After a moment, seemingly resigned to the fact that she wasn't going to get a word out of him, Ms Collier got to the big news. 'I've been talking to your coach and the principal, and we've had an idea. It would be a shame for you to miss the rugby tour; I understand the costs of it are a little high.'

Sione swallowed, his cheeks burning.

'We'd like to announce a mufti day in your honour for this Monday. Every student will be allowed to wear their favourite jersey or team colours instead of the school uniform, the cost being a gold-coin donation towards your travel expenses. I know it isn't much notice, but hopefully all the students will be able to bring some money to help you out. Lots of gold coins can really add up.'

Sione said nothing. He couldn't decide if he felt excited or embarrassed by the whole thing.

'What do you think? Can I call your dad to let him know?'

Sione nodded, and Ms Collier excused herself and left. Immediately, Sione's stomach lurched. He hated that feeling. He wanted to be a part of the Valley rep team more than anything, but not at the cost of becoming the centre of attention. How could he ask all the kids at school to give him money? What if he did get to go on the tour but played terribly? Then he'd be *wasting* everyone's money.

Sione trudged back to his classroom. He walked even slower once he heard the maths lesson that was taking place inside. He tucked Izzy's email safely inside his pocket and went in, face down.

The rest of that afternoon was a haze. At one point, prefects came in to announce the mufti day and even mentioned something about Sione making a speech at the Monday assembly. As everyone in his class talked about what they would wear, Sione's stomach sank.

He didn't want to get up in front of the entire school, let alone speak in front of them.

By the time Sione arrived home, he'd decided he wasn't going to school on Monday. This rep team thing was getting way too big.

On Sunday, Sione lay in bed all evening with his stomach in knots. He listened as his family ate dinner without him, frequently punctuated by his dad bursting out with: 'But he'll miss his own mufti day!'

Sione looked up at the giant poster of Izzy on his wall, and at some point he fell asleep. He slept long but far from deeply. When he got out of bed in the morning his dad had already left for work. Aunty and Mele were eating toast in the kitchen.

'How are you this morning, dear?' his aunt asked.

Sione looked at the clock on the micro-wave. It was nine o'clock, too late to get to school. 'A bit better,' he replied.

'Would you like some toast?'

Sione nodded.

'It's a good sign that you feel like eating again,' his aunt said, getting up.

Mele was bopping up and down in her booster seat as music played in the next room. Sione smiled but was careful not to look too happy. He grimaced and held his stomach when Aunty put the toast in front of him.

'You know,' she said, 'I saw Israel Folau on TV last night.'

Sione looked down at his breakfast, but his ears perked upwards like a cat's at the mention of Izzy's name.

'He was talking about how he's changed sports twice and all the challenges he'd faced doing that, like having to learn new things and meet new people and be on the news every night.' She paused, waiting for a reaction from Sione. 'Anyway, he seems like a great guy. I hope you do get to meet him. I'm proud of anyone who faces their problems rather than hiding or running away.'

Sione coughed on his breakfast, and his aunty got him some milk to drink.

That day, as the kids at school dressed in his honour, Sione read Izzy's email over and over again. What's more, he stuck it on his wall above his bed, right next to the poster, so he might dream about it all night.

If Izzy can do tough things, he told himself, *maybe I can too.*

SIONE

The mufti day turned out to be a success, with the money covering the travel costs. Soon after, Sione received his rep jersey and all the details for the training camp and tour. A week later, Sione found himself standing at the bus stop by the train station with his family, waiting for the bus to take him away for his two-week training camp and then the statewide Junior Rugby Championships.

It was a sunny Saturday morning – winter was clearly on the way out – but Sione couldn't appreciate it. His family was sitting at the bus stop, laughing about something or other while Sione stood as stiff as a board next to the bus-stop sign, refusing to sit with them. There was no way he was missing this bus after all that had happened.

He stared down the open road, and it occurred to him that he wasn't anxious about spending two weeks away from home, rather, he was afraid of getting found out. He was sure that, as soon as training started, everyone would see that he was a fake. Hopefully he would be picked to sit on the reserve bench for every game. Then his talent levels would never be in question, or even required.

I haven't even played rugby in two weeks, he thought to himself as he looked down the road. *I'll stink.*

The bus was going to take Sione and the other selected boys to a conference centre, an hour's drive towards the city. They were to spend three days there, getting to know each other and train under Izzy, before going to the airport late on Monday. After that there would be the tour matches across the country before landing back in his home state – this year's host for the Championships.

Sione's aunt had said over and over again how much fun he was going to have and how lucky he was to visit all those places. Sione's dad had said he wished he could go in Sione's place, and Sione was very tempted to let him.

Sione thought about his schoolmates. They were just starting their school holidays and could spend the next two weeks lounging around at home, relaxing, while he was being forced to go on an adventure. He felt exhausted already.

He leant against the bus-stop sign, watching the road. Suddenly, a square speck appeared on the horizon. It grew and grew until it was clear that the team bus was exactly what it was. Aunty stood up, holding Mele's hand, and Dad followed them to stand next to Sione. Now he wasn't just stressed, he was embarrassed, too. He doubted the other boys would have had their families wait with them like they were little kids.

Aunty hugged Sione, and his dad rubbed his head with his rough workman's hand.

As the bus approached, Sione's mind raced through a hundred different escape options and what people might say if he actually did just turn and run. Then he looked at his aunt and remembered what she had said about Izzy and facing challenges instead of running away. He tightened his fists and stood tall. *I'm going to do this*, he decided. *I'm going to face it and do well. If Izzy can, so can . . . Izzy? Is Israel Folau going to be on this bus?* Sione felt like vomiting all over again.

Mele clapped as the bus slowed to a stop, its brakes hissing. It was a very large coach, painted an ominous black. Sione looked upwards, towards the muffled sound of excited boys. It was hard to see well through the tinted windows, but Sione could make out fingers pressed against the glass, pointing in his direction.

Sione groaned inwardly. He lowered his head and turned to face the front door as it whooshed open. His family gathered around him but Sione didn't move.

A sneaker appeared on the steps of the bus. It was followed by a leg in track pants and a Wallabies polo shirt. Above the shirt was a face that bore a smile that Sione knew only too well. He had traced its outlines and features with his eyes every night before going to bed. His poster had come to life.

Sione's aunt gasped as Israel Folau walked towards them. He headed straight for Sione and held out his hand. 'Hi, you must be Sione,' he said with a smile.

Mele giggled, peering from her hiding spot behind one of Sione's legs. Izzy bent his head to see her and waved, causing her to giggle again. Sione didn't know what to say or do. Mele nudged him and pointed to Izzy's hand, which was still hanging in the air. Sione quickly grasped it, shaking Izzy's hand gently.

Izzy grinned. 'Welcome to the team!'

Sione nodded, trying to think of what to say. 'G-Good morning, Mr Folau.'

'Call me Izzy.'

'Uh, o-okay . . . Izzy.' Sione blinked.

Some other adults wearing the team training gear introduced themselves to Sione's dad and aunt. They were in charge of the tour and looking after the boys but Sione didn't catch their names. His dad handed over some medical forms and emergency phone numbers, and before Sione knew it, he was being squeezed goodbye once again by his aunt and sister. One tear did make it through his eye's defences this time. He was going to miss them. Not just because he loved his family, but because they were familiar and safe.

Izzy directed Sione to the door of the bus after the driver had packed his luggage in the storage bay next to its large wheels. Sione's stomach turned again – he didn't want to go in. *What will the boys think of me?* he wondered.

Gingerly, without a backwards glance, he walked up the steps and stood at the front of the bus, scanning the space as a dozen or more pairs of eyes looked back at him. He spotted a seat by the window and imagined swinging his backpack onto the rack above it and hiding himself behind his headphones, alone, until they got to the camp.

But then Izzy climbed the steps behind Sione and spoke to the bus full of kids. 'Everyone, this is Sione. He plays wing for Valley.'

All the other boys immediately began to holler and stamp their feet. The tour leaders behind Sione started clapping their welcome, and soon the whole bus filled with the sound of applause.

Just like that, Sione felt like a part of the team.

DANIEL

Daniel sat at the bus stop, trying to tune out his dad, who had spent the past hour going on and on about what an important day this was and how it was a stepping stone towards Daniel playing for Australia. It wasn't that Daniel didn't agree with him, it was just that he was trying to focus.

Last year, a sports psychologist had visited the school and given a talk at assembly. He'd said it was important to stay focused in all areas of life – school and sport. The psychologist had talked about what some famous athletes did before a big match to get themselves in the zone.

Many sports stars listen to music before a game to keep calm, or have a very specific warm-up routine. Some of them even do yoga. Daniel had decided the music option was the one for him. It would keep him focused as he thought about the big two weeks in front of him and all he had to prove. Plus, he'd look so cool walking onto the bus while holding the latest phone. But his dad had said it was rude to have headphones on while someone was talking to you, so the phone was in his pocket.

Daniel knew that from the moment he sat down in the bus, he wanted to be the leader, not a follower. He was certain that his rugby prowess made him ready for the job as a representative player, but projecting himself into the role of captain – *that* would be what would set him apart on this tour.

'Just don't forget that this isn't the end of the road,' his dad said. 'The job of the selectors is never over. They'll be watching this team, too, looking for the players they think will best represent the entire state at the end of the year. You'll have to fight for your spot on that team every year until you're an adult and aiming for the Wallabies.'

Daniel nodded absently. He had heard this speech a hundred times. Every night at dinner his dad would talk to him about leadership and playing for the Wallabies and everything else. Daniel loved hearing he was destined for greatness, but he'd heard all his dad had to say already. He hoped that Israel Folau might be able to mentor him in a more direct manner.

Daniel thought back to the assembly the week before and the email from Izzy that the headmaster had read out. What Izzy had said about having fun excited him. It was a refreshing change from what he usually heard.

'Here it comes!'

Daniel stood up as soon as his dad spoke, and approached the kerb. The coach was large and black, with dark, tinted windows. It looked to Daniel like an enormous limo and that made him feel special. He could see excited boys peering out at him and pointing in his direction.

'It seems your fame has preceded you,' his dad laughed.

Daniel walked up to the front door as it opened. His dad wished him good luck and Daniel put his foot on the bottom step. Looking up, he saw the great Israel Folau walking down the few steps to meet him.

'Hi,' Izzy said with a smile. 'You must be Daniel.'

'That's me,' Daniel replied.

'Welcome to the tour,' Izzy said. 'It's so great to have you!'

Daniel smiled back at his idol. 'Thanks.'

'You can get on the bus if you like. I just need to introduce the staff to your dad.'

Daniel decided to step back off the coach to watch Izzy and three other adults in the Valley gear come out to shake hands with his dad.

'Nice to meet you, Israel,' his dad said.

'You too, but please call me Izzy.' They shook hands, and Izzy introduced the others as Daniel looked on, one hand on the bus's doorhandle. 'This is Jeremy Fisk. He's the tour manager, getting us everywhere we need to go to on time. This is Tom and Mary Parker, who will be looking after all the boys' needs. They'll be the ones who'll call you if we need anything.'

'Fine, fine, nice to meet you,' Daniel's dad said briskly. He pointed at his son. 'He's some player. You'll be amazed at what he can do.'

Mr Fisk smiled and nodded. 'Every boy that was selected was chosen because they have special talents.'

'Not quite like Daniel's, I'm sure,' Mr Masters countered. He waved goodbye as Daniel climbed onto the bus and put on his headphones.

'Everyone,' Izzy announced at the top of the stairs, 'this is Daniel. He plays fly-half for Valley. He's a great goal kicker, too.' Everyone clapped and cheered, and Daniel nodded. It seemed that they all loved him already. This was going to be sweet.

The seats on the coach were in rows, two seats on either side of the aisle. They had high backs, curtains at the windows and reading lights. It was almost as good as a plane.

Daniel chose the chair behind Izzy so he could get close to his new coach right from the start. He put his bag on the luggage rack above and settled into his chair with his music playing soft enough that he could still hear everything.

Some boys were chatting up the back but otherwise it was a very quiet bus. Daniel assumed it was because no one knew each other. He looked across the aisle and saw another boy sitting just like him, headphones on, minding his own business. The bus moved out of the bus stop and Izzy announced that there were only three more players to collect before heading off to the conference centre.

There were a few small TVs hanging from the ceiling at various points and a movie the boys had been watching flicked back on. Some were watching it intently, but Daniel ignored it. He had to focus.

Daniel looked back at the other boy, sizing him up. He was tall and thin, probably a winger. Daniel racked his brain for a way to begin a conversation with Izzy, who was now sitting just centimetres away.

Izzy turned, but instead of talking to Daniel, he called out to the other boy across from him. 'Sione!' he said. The boy turned his head cautiously. 'Tongan?' The boy called Sione smiled and nodded. 'Me too,' Izzy said.

'Yeah – I know,' Sione replied sheepishly.

Izzy turned back to look out the window and so did Sione. Daniel sank low in his seat. He was behind in the score already.

'Um, excuse me, Israel,' he said through the seats.

'Izzy,' came the reply with a chuckle.

'I just wanted to say thank you for the email you sent. My headmaster read it out at assembly. I thought it was great.'

Izzy turned to face Daniel over the back of his seat. 'My pleasure. I'm glad you liked it. It would be great to win, all I can ask is that we do our best and enjoy ourselves along the way.'

Daniel nodded. This was awesome! Izzy was awesome!

The bus pulled to another stop, and as Izzy and the other adults welcomed the next player to the team, the rest of the boys started chatting, looking through their windows and pointing. Some were guessing what position the new boy outside played.

'Flanker,' a boy said. 'We've only got one so far. Or second row, maybe.'

Daniel stood up to look at him. He knelt on the seat next to Sione and peered over his shoulder. He saw a regular-looking boy standing next to his parents, talking to Izzy and the others. Then the boy's mother bent over and kissed him on the cheek. Daniel laughed. This made Sione look up at him.

'Your mum doesn't still kiss you, does she?' he asked. When he didn't get a reply, Daniel shrugged his shoulders and returned to his seat.

The new boy climbed on the bus with Izzy, who announced, 'Hey guys, this is Tim. He plays second row and I hear he is a great goal kicker, too.'

Everyone clapped and cheered loudly, except for Daniel, who didn't make a sound. *Another goal kicker?* he fumed. *And the clapping is for everyone?*

Hunching down in his seat, Daniel turned up the volume and glared out the window.

SIONE

Music blared in Sione's ears as he read Izzy's email for the hundredth time. He still couldn't believe that Izzy had taken the time to write to him. Over the past week he had taken to reading the letter whenever he felt sad or anxious. Somehow it made him feel special, knowing that one of the greatest rugby players in the world knew who he was.

He looked over at Izzy sitting diagonally in front of him, and chuckled to himself. He was still so excited by Izzy's letter that he hadn't fully taken in the fact that Izzy himself was riding on the same bus!

The boy across the aisle shot him a quizzical look. His face seemed to say, 'What's up with you?', before he looked down at his pockets and began emptying them onto the seat next to him.

Chocolate after chocolate, lolly after lolly appeared, and by the time he was done there was a pyramid the size of which the ancient Egyptians would have been proud of. The boy rummaged through his pile until he found the bag of lollies he was looking for.

Sione couldn't help but watch. He hadn't

even thought to bring any junk food, wanting to look healthy in front of Izzy. This boy, on the other hand, seemed to be taking pride in all that he had.

The boy noticed Sione watching and sighed. Reluctantly, he held out his bag. 'Want one?' he asked.

Sione didn't. The taste of toothpaste was still in his mouth and he didn't think its mintiness would mix well with the sour cola lollies he was being offered. But he took one anyway and said thank you so as not to hurt the boy's feelings.

'What do you play?' the boy asked next.

Sione, struggling to enjoy the rubbery lolly, answered though glassy eyes and clenched teeth. 'Rugby.'

'I know that!' the boy snorted. 'I meant, what position do you play?'

Sione blushed. 'Wing.'

'Are you a goal kicker as well?'

'No.'

'That's good.' The boy smiled. 'I think it's bad for morale to have too many people try out for the same positions.' He swallowed a mouthful of lollies without flinching and said, 'My name's Daniel. I play fly-half.'

'I'm Sione. I play wing.'

'Yeah, you already said that.'

Sione knew that the rules of conversation said that it was now his turn to come up with a question or snappy comment to keep the discussion going. He hated it when this happened. Why couldn't the other person just keep talking? After a long pause, he came up with something. 'Who do you play for?' he asked in a tiny voice.

'Huh?'

'Who do you play for?' Sione repeated.

Daniel looked at him, puzzled. 'I play for my school. Don't you?'

Sione shook his head. He had no idea you could play rugby at your school, and certainly not regularly enough to get rep selection. He wanted to ask how long Daniel's lunchbreak was that they could fit in official matches, but his instincts told him this would not be a good follow-up question.

'I go to Barton Grammar,' Daniel added. 'What about you?'

Sione had never heard of that school. It

didn't even sound like the name of a school to him.

'Valley North?' Sione squeaked.

Daniel snorted. 'Does Valley North have lots of rugby players?'

Sione wasn't sure what Daniel was asking. 'Tonnes of people love it,' he said. 'I play on the grass pretty much every lunchtime.'

Daniel's eyebrows lowered. *'That's* how you were selected for Valley? Mucking around at lunchtime? What sort of standards do these selectors have?'

'No, no,' Sione said, waving a hand. 'I play for the Tigers in the local competition. We train at Henderson Oval near the swimming pool – you know the place? We play proper games every Saturday or Sunday. We wear uniforms and everything.'

'Huh. To tell you the truth, I was expecting everyone here to come from the schools comp. I didn't think the level of the club rugby was that high.'

Sione wasn't sure exactly what Daniel was talking about, but he wasn't going to try and guess. He had just said more words to a stranger than he ever had in his life and he felt exhausted.

To Sione, Daniel was his total opposite. His rugby experiences were of a type unknown to him, and it seemed Daniel was thinking of Sione in a similar way. It was more than awkward for him, but deep down Sione realised he was liking the idea of this trip much more now. Meeting people who lived close by but whose life stories were so different was interesting. He looked at Izzy, who smiled back. Had he heard the conversation? Sione hoped not.

Sione's very first day at rugby training felt similar to this. His dad had taken him along because Sione had said he wanted to join a team. But when he'd walked onto the field that first time, his desire was immediately replaced by fear. All the other boys already knew each other. The coach was joking around with them when his dad introduced him to the group. For some reason that had embarrassed Sione, and he had felt extra shy once he realised there were no Tongan boys on the team. No one talked to him and he didn't talk back. Everything felt foreign.

There were two reasons alone why Sione didn't ask to go home right there and then. First, he didn't want to disappoint his dad. Second, once the training drills began, Sione felt somehow free from the stares. He let his feet do the talking and he ran all over that field, chasing balls and tackling padding until he was drained of all energy. Sione made his own fun and he had never felt prouder than after that first session, gulping down some much-deserved water as his new coach sang his praises to his dad.

That was the feeling he had strived for at every training session since. 'Push yourself so that you can feel proud and enjoy that bottle of water,' was something he was continually telling himself.

'I guess they have to share things around and give everyone a go,' Daniel said, half to himself, bringing Sione back to the present. 'By giving some spots to the clubs, I mean.' He looked at Sione. 'Some people play well off the bench – that's what my dad says.'

'Some do,' Izzy said, turning to face Daniel. 'And some champions have come from the most unexpected places.'

Daniel turned around. 'Have you ever played off the bench?' he asked Izzy.

'Of course.'

'Where did you play when you were a kid? What school did you go to?'

'Minto.'

'Where's that?'

'My home, in Sydney,' Izzy answered.

'But who you play for isn't as important as *how* you play. Did you know that even players from teams at the bottom of the ladder can be selected for Australia?'

'Yeah, but it's rare,' Daniel said, now sucking on a lollipop.

'That's a lot of sugar for an athlete,' Izzy laughed. 'We won't be allowing junk food on tour, just so you know. You can only be the best you can be if you eat right.'

Daniel pulled the lollipop from his mouth with a *pop*. 'Sorry,' he said, not sounding sorry at all.

'No problem,' Izzy said, breaking into a wide smile. He looked over at Sione. 'The most important thing isn't where you started, but where you finish,' he said.

Soon after, the bus pulled up to the conference centre, which was to be the boys' home for the next two nights. It had cabins, a central building with a dining room and a big hall, and a large rugby field at the back.

'This is it, guys,' Izzy called. 'Time to get your things and get settled in. We are now officially on tour!'

DANIEL

The boys stood outside the bus in a straight line as Mary Parker went down the line, counting by twos. There were twenty boys in total. *Enough for five reserves*, Daniel thought, telling himself that there was no way he would become one of them.

'There are seven cabins for us,' Mary

announced. 'They back onto the rugby field, so we'll be nice and close to it for our training sessions. Four boys to a cabin, two cabins for the adults.

'Before we take you to your cabins, there are a few rules you need to know. There may be other groups staying here, so no loud noises or playing around the other cabins. Also, there is a games room and swimming pool in the main building, but please don't go there right now – or without one of the adults – this time is about getting settled in our rooms. In half an hour we will meet back here and talk more about the weekend.'

'Oh, and the snack machines are out of bounds, too,' Jeremy Fisk added, and all the boys groaned.

Tom Parker laughed. 'Don't worry, we will feed you very well.'

They walked in single file towards the first cabin. Some boys were passing footballs to each other as they walked.

'Eric, Joseph, Steven and TJ,' Mary said, pointing to its open door. The four boys rushed inside excitedly.

At the next cabin, another four boys cheered and high-fived when their names were read aloud. Clearly, they all knew each other. Daniel made a mental note to find out who they played for – having four from the same team went against his theory that they had shared the selections around.

Then came the third cabin. Daniel's name was called and he was inside before the other three names were even read out. As he entered, the bathroom was on his left, and in front was the main bedroom that consisted of one double bed and two sets of bunk beds. Daniel immediately threw his bag on the double bed and looked around for the TV that wasn't there.

In walked his three roommates. The first two he hadn't met yet, but the boy at the back was Sione from the bus. 'Hey, guys,' he said, nodding at the first two. 'I'm Daniel, the fly-half.'

'I'm Jake,' said the first.

'Adam,' said the second.

'How come you have the big bed?' Jake asked, pointing at Daniel's bag. He was a huge boy who looked too old for the team. He was tall and wider than both Daniel and Sione put together. His question took Daniel by surprise.

'What do you mean?' he said. 'I was here first.'

'That's just because they read out your name first,' Jake said. 'You should have waited to talk about it.'

'I was here second!' Adam said. He sprawled across the double bed, next to Daniel's bag.

'Hey, that's my bed!' Daniel snapped.

Jake and Adam laughed. Sione put his bag next to one of the bottom bunks and lay on it, his hands behind his head, waiting for the storm to blow over.

Daniel thought about his desire to be team captain and searched his mind for a clever compromise. 'How about no one gets the bed? There are enough bunks.'

Jake nodded and threw his bag on the top bunk on the other side of the room, and Adam threw his on its bottom level. Daniel turned to look at Sione, then looked at the empty bunk bed above him. *Well, at least I've got a top bunk*, he thought to himself.

The boys unpacked their belongings and placed them on the double bed. 'This can be our display table,' Daniel said. Soon, everything that the boys would be needing semi-regularly over the weekend was neatly laid out upon it instead of being tucked away in their luggage. Their four Valley jerseys were given pride of place, folded neatly along the top of the bed.

The boys then started checking out each other's football gear – the brands, colours and appearance of each boot, sock and mouthguard. Daniel found his headgear and placed it neatly on his jersey to finish his unpacking.

'You wear headgear?' Adam asked.

'Yeah, Dad wants me to wear it 'cause I took a big knock a couple of years ago,' Daniel replied. 'Anyway, it makes me stand out on the field.'

Jake picked it up and tried to slide it over his head but it didn't fit. The boys laughed as he pranced around with it on his way-too-big head.

'Lucky it's green,' Adam commented. 'Valley colours.'

Daniel shrugged. 'My school's colours are green and white. Who do you guys play for? What school?'

'I go to St Christopher's,' Adam said proudly.

'I'm at Queens,' Jake said.

'Who do you play for again?' Daniel asked Sione.

Sione sat up and took the headphones out of his ears. 'Huh?'

Daniel turned back to the others. 'He doesn't go to a rugby school. He plays for a club – the Tigers?'

'Yeah.' Sione nodded and pointed at his pile of training gear on the double bed. Everything was orange and black.

'Cool,' Adam said.

Jake gestured to the wall behind Sione. 'What's that?' he asked.

'Nothing,' Sione said quickly.

A folded piece of paper was stuck to the wall. Jake walked over to Sione's bed to take a closer look. 'It's the email Izzy sent to all of us.'

'You kept it?' Adam said, laughing.

Daniel smirked. 'We all got that. I didn't even keep a copy.'

'I know, right?' The other two laughed.

Sione shrugged, his cheeks flushed. 'I like it,' he said, softly but defiantly.

The boys stood outside listening to the plan for the rest of their stay. They had free time before dinner, followed by team-building exercises in the hall. Daniel grunted. That didn't seem interesting at all.

'After that,' Tom announced, 'Izzy is going to show you some rugby video clips and discuss them with you.'

'Woo!' Daniel howled. That was more his style!

Tom threw him a warning look. 'Tomorrow is training all day, starting after breakfast. I'll tell you more about that later but there's all sorts of things planned. We'll have a practice game or two on Monday before we head to the airport.'

'When do we have to go to bed tonight?' asked one of the boys.

'Lights out at nine-thirty sharp.'

'What?' Daniel exclaimed, horrified. 'That's way early!'

'Trust me — with all the work we have to do tomorrow, you'll need the rest,' Izzy said from behind the crowd. Everyone turned to face him. 'I can't have you guys falling asleep on the field, can I?' he added, laughing heartily.

Daniel hung his head. This camp was starting to sound more like a punishment than a reward.

'Remember that we aren't here to have a party,' Jeremy added. 'You are all being taught the importance of teamwork and commitment – qualities you need if you are to be a rugby champion.'

Daniel frowned, confused. The messages he was getting on this trip about rugby were nothing like his dad's advice.

At dinner, Daniel sat with Adam and Jake and they talked the whole time about their schools, teams and the amazing tries they'd scored. Afterwards, Tom, Mary and

Izzy took the boys through a series of team-building games. For some of the activities, Daniel was paired up with Sione, who, in his opinion, was the worst teammate *ever*. When Daniel was blindfolded and being led around an obstacle course, Sione kept bumping him into things. When they had to answer trivia questions, Sione always got them wrong. When they had to solve problems, Sione just got confused.

Each activity scored the partnerships points, and after finishing last in the rankings for the night, Daniel had had enough. 'This isn't rugby,' he complained loudly.

Izzy sighed. 'No, it isn't,' he said. 'But if you can't work together off the field, how will you cooperate when you're on it?'

Daniel glared at Sione. It was a good thing he'd be far away on the wing and out of trouble.

SIONE

Sione was roused early the next morning by the sound of kookaburras singing outside his cabin. He tucked his hands behind his head and watched the room gradually brighten as the sun's rays slipped inside. He lay there for what felt like hours, listening to the mattress above him creak with Daniel's every move and Jake's snores.

Sione wasn't sure why everyone always wanted the top bunk; he preferred the bottom. It was like a private room, with a roof and a wall. He turned to the wall and looked at the email from Izzy. He didn't know why he'd hung onto it; all he knew was it made him feel special and want to play well.

Perhaps it was also a source of comfort. Sione was feeling more and more out of place on the camp. Last night, many of the boys – including Jake, Adam and Daniel – had dressed up in nice clothes for dinner. They'd done their hair and sprayed deodorant. It was like they all knew they should do it, while Sione just walked into the dining room in his tracksuit. No one said anything, but Sione knew what they were all thinking.

All they ate was plain old spaghetti bolognaise, but the others had treated it like a meal in a fancy restaurant. *Is this a chance to learn and play great rugby, or a popularity contest?* Sione had wondered.

And the less said about the team games and training videos the better. Daniel had spent the night complaining about how inferior a partner Sione was. Sione had been hurt and confused by it all. Daniel had been the one who seemed to sabotage all their attempts to succeed, but by vocalising that Sione was to blame, everyone had joined in with Daniel and pointed fingers at him. He had only wanted to have some fun, but as soon as it was clear they weren't going to win the events, Daniel just gave up.

During the video session, Izzy had shown some famous tries from the last couple of World Cups. After each clip, Izzy asked the boys how the try was scored. Daniel would call out the answer every time, yelling things like, 'The cut-out pass threw the defence off guard' or 'The brute strength of the forwards pushed him over'. Each time Izzy would say that he was partly correct, but that it was teamwork that had really resulted in the tries.

'The whole team has to work together to be on the same page,' Izzy had said, 'and each member can't be worried about taking the limelight for themselves.'

Sione had loved this lesson while Daniel kept snorting his disagreement, even after Izzy had pointed out how the things that players without the ball were doing affected the player running with it.

Sione was getting cross just thinking about it. He got out of bed and jumped in the shower. By the time Sione had left the bathroom, washed and dressed, it was still an hour before breakfast and the other three boys were still asleep. Quietly, Sione grabbed his hoodie off the double bed and left the room to go for a walk.

The crisp morning air was refreshing and Sione smiled at the way the bright sunshine made the leaves in the trees sparkle. The kookaburras' laughing had been replaced by other birdsongs now, and Sione shielded his eyes from the sun with his hood and set out for the rugby field.

Before every Tigers game, Sione liked to walk a couple of laps of the field, thinking about the game and how it might go. With the first training session only a couple of hours away, Sione wasn't sure he'd get the opportunity, so now seemed like a good time to get to know the posts, line markings and pitch before he would be expected to perform upon it.

He walked between two cabins and through some bushes before emerging onto a field. It was a simple rectangle of grass with the familiar white posts at each end of it. Bordered all around by trees and cabins, the space seemed enclosed – private and special.

But Sione wasn't alone. At the far end of the pitch, he spied a familiar figure sprinting back and forth between the tryline and the 22-yard line. It was Izzy, in a green-and-gold training top and white boots, huffing and puffing. Sione watched from a distance as Izzy gulped down some water before switching to a jumping and skipping drill, moving up and down the touchline. He watched in silence for a long time, half-thinking the right thing to do would be to give his coach some privacy, the other half wanting to learn how champions train.

Sione was proud that he had Izzy Folau as a mentor – someone who led by example, rather than with hollow words or power.

When Izzy had finished, he stretched on the grass and finished the rest of his water.

'Oh, hey, Sione,' he said with a wave, finally noticing his single spectator.

'Hey,' Sione replied. 'Sorry.'

'There's no need to apologise. You can join me tomorrow morning, if you like.'

Sione's jaw dropped. 'Um, okay,' he said.

Izzy walked over. 'I want to keep up with my training, and mornings are really the only time I have on tour. How have you found the camp so far?'

'Okay,' Sione replied. He hoped he didn't sound ungrateful.

'I'm sure it will be great fun, but I know how hard it is to start somewhere new,' Izzy said, wiping his forehead with a towel. 'Did you know rugby union is my third sport?'

Sione nodded.

'Each time I've faced a new challenge it has been really hard, but I've had great times and learnt so much. I think you will, too.'

Sione smiled. 'That's why my aunty likes you so much,' he said.

Izzy laughed. 'Next time you speak to her, tell your aunty that I'm very flattered.'

After a hearty breakfast, the boys hit the rugby field for the first time as a group. Most boys came with the expectation they would be doing skills training or position work, but the first session was purely based on fitness. Izzy took the boys through a full warm-up routine, a set of runs and finished off with a beep test. At the very mention of the beep test, most of the other players groaned, Daniel moaning the loudest of all. Sione, too shy to say he didn't know what a beep test was, listened intently to Izzy's explanation. He learnt that this test was made up of a series of back-and-forth sprints that are timed with beeps. Runners were given less and less time to complete each run the further they progressed. If a boy didn't make his mark before the beep sounded, he was knocked out of the test and given a score.

With each turn, Sione pictured Izzy earlier that morning, pushing himself to do his best, even though no one was watching. Sione was so deep in thought he was oblivious to the other boys dropping out around him, to

Daniel's complaints when he was knocked out, and to the fact that, eventually, the group of runners had dwindled down to just him and TJ.

Cheers rang out after every completed lap, rousing Sione from his thoughts. He couldn't believe it. Boys were clapping for him, encouraging him to keep going.

Then TJ was gone and it was just him left. How he made each mark before the beeps, Sione didn't know. Each sprint was now incredibly fast and his heart was beating rapidly. Worse than that, though, was the heavy feeling in his thighs and calves. *Just one more*, he thought. *No regrets.*

Beep . . . beep . . .

'Just one more!'

Cheers rained down when the current speed was announced. Sione collapsed on the ground, hands patting him from every direction.

'Try and stand up, Sione,' he heard Izzy say, as if from the other end of a tunnel. 'You'll recover quicker. Hands on your head.'

Sione did as he was told. He was shocked at his ability and proud of his drive. There would be no regrets for him today. Adam handed him a bottle of water and it tasted like liquid gold.

There was a break for morning tea and a little free time before everyone was expected back on the field for some drills. The others continued to congratulate Sione, though he tried to keep a low profile. As great as the beep test had been, he knew that the next session, when he would actually have to show some playing skills, was the real test.

The boys were split into backs and forwards. As there were a few too many players, Izzy planned to interchange them regularly. Due to his morning's efforts, Sione was picked to be left wing first. The drill was set up – a simple one so Izzy could see the team in motion. The forwards had to form a scrum around a scrum machine as the backs stretched out along the field behind them.

Daniel found the ball and smiled so wide Sione could see it from the other side of the field. Had he practised this recently? Daniel threw the ball to Harrison, the scrum-half, and gave him a high five.

Sione watched as Harrison fed the ball into the semi-scrum. He enjoyed these moments of solitude on the field, all the way out near the far touchline on his own. He set himself, watching and waiting . . .

And then the ball came free. The backs quickly advanced in a line, ensuring that they didn't move in front of the players to their right. The ball flew along the row of backs. Soon it would be in Sione's hands.

Tom, Mary, Jeremy and Izzy were applauding the ball's progress from somewhere behind him. It was now with the boy at outside centre. Sione was next.

The ball was passed to Sione, but with much more force than he was expecting. It came at him like a spinning dart. It went through his hands and punched him in the chest with its point.

Sione exhaled and stumbled to the ground. 'Ugh!'

The ball bounced over the touchline and into a bush. The other nineteen boys groaned, and Sione's stomach plummeted.

DANIEL

The day before had been extremely tiring but lots of fun. They had done so much work on the field that Daniel had fallen asleep before lights out, and it had been a great feeling to wake up on Monday morning, knowing that his deep rest had been well deserved.

The Sunday highlights for Daniel would definitely have been the amazing roast dinner and movie night, but the display of his bunk mate on the training pitch was something he couldn't get out of his head.

Sione had been popular in the morning when all they had been doing was running. But when the rugby balls came out, Daniel saw it was a different story. Sione had totally fallen apart. He couldn't catch anything, and most repetitions and drills stopped short whenever he went near the play.

Daniel wasn't sure why Sione had been so nervous. After training was finally over, Sione had disappeared to the shower but Daniel had stayed out and practised his goal kicking, just

as he did after every session. Izzy congratulated him on his extra effort, which filled him
with pride.

When he had eventually returned to their
cabin, Sione had been even quieter than usual.
Daniel supposed he had learnt that schoolboy
rugby was better.

Now it was Monday and, for Daniel, the day
had an aura of excitement about it. Not only
were they heading to the airport after lunch,
but Izzy had scheduled practice matches for
the morning session. Daniel was really looking
forward to it so he could properly show off his
captaincy skills.

After breakfast, the boys gathered around
Izzy at the halfway line. Sione stood back
from the main group as he listened.

Daniel wanted him to stand with them, the way a teammate should. *You've got to learn to take this game by the horns, Sione*, Daniel wanted to say. *Don't be afraid or you'll never get better.*

Sione's eyes met Daniel's for a split second before he looked down again.

'So this is how it's going to work,' Izzy began. 'It's ten to a side, with twenty-minute halves. After one game we will have a break, mix you up and go again. With less players, some of you will have to play altered positions – the scrum will be smaller, the back line shorter – but you'll have more space and time to do all your magic tricks.' Izzy winked at Daniel, who attached his chin strap to show he was ready. 'Show me everything you've got, and remember to have some fun!'

The boys were then split into two even teams, with Sione and Daniel on opposite sides. Daniel gathered all his teammates around him. 'Good luck, guys,' he said. 'I'm the only kicker here, so I'll do all that. We don't really know each other yet, so we may make mistakes, but don't worry. Listen to my instructions if you aren't sure what we should do.'

Jake and Adam rolled their eyes but said nothing.

In a moment, they were standing along the halfway line as Daniel prepared to kick off. Izzy blew the whistle, and Daniel kicked the ball with pinpoint accuracy towards Sione. He was standing in the right corner of the field, and as the ball screamed towards him, his legs seemed to wobble like jelly and his arms awkwardly shot up to try and catch the ball.

'Catch it!' his teammates cried.

The ball sank and, instead of taking it on the full, Sione decided to let it bounce first. But it didn't come to him. The ball hit the grass and shot off at a right angle, over the touchline. There would now be a line-out, just metres from Daniel's tryline.

Players came over to pat Daniel on the back, congratulating him on the kick. With giant Jake on their side, the line-out was theirs for the taking. No one went to congratulate Sione this time.

Jake won the line-out, jumping high with Adam's support, and after a beautiful, long set-up pass from Daniel, TJ scored a try under the posts. Daniel kicked the conversion easily, bringing the score to 7–0 within a couple of minutes.

'Don't worry, B Team,' Izzy called, 'this is just a practice match and the scores don't count. I want to hear more talk, though, okay?'

There *was* more talk from the other team after that, but from what Daniel could hear, it was all directed at Sione and it didn't sound positive.

As the game continued, Daniel noticed that most of the defensive pressure was aimed at him and he loved that. Yes, it made things more difficult to have multiple, big forwards bearing down on you at every moment, but it meant that they were afraid of him, that he was playing well. As Daniel's dad often said, it was the ultimate compliment to have a team worried about you.

At the end of the forty minutes, Izzy began by reminding everyone that the score was irrelevant and he hadn't taken notice. But Daniel had. His team had won 31–5, with Daniel kicking five out of five attempts and setting up three tries. Tim, the goal kicker on the other side, had missed his only attempt. Daniel was more than pleased with his performance.

With fewer players, there hadn't been as much tackling, rucking and mauling as one would normally expect in a game but everyone was still feeling banged up and ready for a rest. The only thing that kept them wanting to play the second game was the desire to impress.

After a cool-down, sandwiches and then another warm-up, the boys positioned themselves on the two sides of the field for the second practice match. This time Daniel and Sione were on the same team.

'If the ball is kicked to you,' Daniel said in Sione's direction, 'either catch it or get out of the way so someone else can.'

Sione hung his head and walked over to his side of the field.

There was no pep talk this time. Daniel was sure everyone knew to follow his lead. But before kicking off, he saw Izzy talking to Sione quietly. Daniel grimaced and looked away. *I should be the one getting the attention,* he thought. *Can't Izzy see all the good things I'm doing?*

The game began and the teams were clearly more evenly matched this time. There was no score in the first half, just lots of bumps and bruises as players struggled to gain some kind of advantage. At one point the ball was stuck in a small zone of Daniel's half for what seemed like forever. In an attempt to break the deadlock after his teammates had regained possession of the ball from a furious rucking contest, Daniel screamed for it and promptly kicked the ball high and down field – about forty metres towards his scoring end – and out of bounds. Even Izzy cheered him after that.

The ball came back into play, was passed down the back line, and when Sione actually managed to receive a pass, it looked certain the team would score. Sione broke expertly through two defenders and was clear, but instead of heading straight for the tryline, he cut back inside towards the goalposts. There, he found Jake waiting for him.

Sione went down and the scoring opportunity disappeared. He placed the ball behind him in the tackle and Daniel picked it up, passing it to Adam, who passed it on to TJ. It was he, with the defence in disarray, who scored in the corner on the other side of the pitch.

'Look, see that?' Daniel shouted at Sione in frustration. 'Next time, just go for the line. Sometimes there's no room to be fancy.'

Sione clenched his teeth and stared at Daniel. 'I was trying to help the team, okay? You aren't the coach! Just leave me alone!'

The other players were stunned speechless. It was the most they'd heard Sione say, and certainly the loudest his voice had ever been these past three days.

Izzy ran over, a concerned look on his face. 'Hey, guys, calm down! What's up?'

'He keeps picking on me,' Sione said, hating the whine in his voice.

'No, I don't. I'm just trying to help,' Daniel shot back, shaking his head.

'I'm sure you are just trying to help,' Izzy said gently, 'but remember that Sione is trying his best. He wants to play well.'

Daniel knew Izzy was right, but it didn't stop him from feeling frustrated. He wanted Sione to focus and to play like a rep. He had only been trying to wake him up.

'Sorry,' Sione said softly. 'I'm just stressed out about not playing well.'

'I'm sorry too,' Daniel said grudgingly. 'I need to say things nicer, I guess.'

The ball was thrown from somewhere and bounced at Daniel's feet. He took it and set up his conversion kick, glad to get out of the awkward conversation. It was a tough kick from all the way out near touch. It got enough height but didn't move in the air nearly as much as it needed to, sailing well clear of the nearest post.

Daniel kicked his tee in disgust. Arguing with Sione must have put him off. He stared at him in frustration. He wasn't sorry at all. Why was Sione even on this team?

The second half was as tight as the first, but both teams managed tries. The tie was broken in the eighteenth minute by Sione, who scored a lucky try under the posts. Daniel didn't watch, but he did kick the conversion so hard it got stuck high in a tree.

'All right, let's end the game there,' Izzy said. 'You all deserve an early mark. Hit the showers and then we'll have lunch. We'll discuss these games as a group after that.'

While most of the boys were revelling in the experience, Daniel felt nothing but anger and frustration.

'Daniel, Sione,' Izzy called out before they could leave. Both boys trudged over to him, dreading what was to come. 'There's no need to look so down, guys – you both played great, and I'm glad you're on the Valley team. I think this is going to be a terrific tour.'

'But?' Daniel said.

Izzy smiled. 'There are no buts. I've changed sports a few times, and every time

I did there were people who weren't happy. Without meaning to, I upset fans, the media and, worst of all, my teammates. Each time I had to walk into a change room filled with people I didn't know to play a game I wasn't too sure about. I found it hard to be happy and relaxed sometimes, but I did my best to make it work. I trained, I was nice to people, I was a good teammate. You know why?'

'Why?' Daniel asked.

'If I didn't, I might as well have gone home. It's the same for you guys. If you can't chill out, have fun and be proud of your achievements, then you might as well think about going home. Though, I'm pretty sure neither of you want to do that.'

Daniel laughed at the idea. 'No way,' he said.

Sione exhaled loudly, and Daniel and Izzy both turned to look at him. As frustrated as Daniel had felt with Sione, he didn't want to hear him say he'd had enough of the tour.

'I don't know how to get home from here, anyway,' Sione said after a long pause, and all three of them burst into laughter.

With that, Daniel and Sione walked back to their cabin side by side, a fresh start in the air.

SIONE

You might as well go home. The words echoed in Sione's head as he showered and changed. He could hear the other boys in his room joking around. Part of him wished he was friendly enough with them to join in. The other half of him wished they'd just go away.

133

He got his mobile out of the bag under his bed, sneakily sliding it into a pocket in his track pants before leaving the room. He knew that if the others saw his beat-up, old pre-paid phone it would just be one more thing for Daniel to put him down about.

Sione walked back to the rugby field. It was five minutes before lunch, so he didn't have long. Quickly, he dialled the only phone number he knew off by heart.

'Hi, it's me,' he said when his aunty answered.

'It's Sione! Mele, Vili, come say hello! You're okay, right?' she said.

'Yes,' Sione answered. It felt kind of weird talking to her. He hadn't been gone from home very long, but it felt like his family was in another country. He could imagine Mele hopping down the hallway towards the phone and he felt so homesick he almost cried.

'Hi, Sione!' his sister yelled, breathing heavily into the phone.

Sione smiled. 'Hey.'

'Guess what? Dad said I can get a puppy! Soon, when I'm ten.'

Sione laughed. 'But that's, like, six years away.'

'It's soon!' his little sister insisted.

'Sione doesn't want to talk about puppies,' he could hear his aunt say in the background. 'Give the phone to your dad.'

'Bye, Sione!' Mele called before the slow, familiar voice of his father took over.

'How's it going, son? Have you played yet?' his dad asked.

'Yeah, just training and practice matches, though.'

'Going good?'

'I guess.'

'Good boy. Make sure you have fun. We'll be there to see you at the Championships in a couple of weeks, yeah? Terry's coming, too.'

'Okay.'

'Call if you need.'

'Yep.'

'We're very proud of you, Sione,' his aunt said. 'Just do your best and remember to have fun – you'll never forget this experience.'

How did Aunty do that? She always seemed

to know what Sione needed to hear. 'Okay,' he said before saying goodbye.

Sione returned the phone to his pocket and wiped his eyes. Somehow, that three-minute phone call had given him his strength back. His on-field mistakes seemed miles away. He ran back to his cabin, grabbed his favourite cap and hurried off after his teammates.

That afternoon, after a final chat from Izzy about the team, it was time to pack and head to the airport. Sione couldn't wait for the next stage of their journey. This weekend had been tough, but Sione could already see it had been worth it. *Who knows?* he thought. *I might even become friends with some of the boys.*

While the others took their time packing, Sione decided to make one last visit to the rugby field. As he passed between the last row of cabins, the kookaburras began laughing and, once again, there was a lone figure training on the pitch.

But it wasn't Izzy this time, it was Daniel. He was practising his goal kicking in his regular clothes and football boots. Sione watched him place the ball on the tee before looking. Their eyes met, and Daniel froze. Sione didn't know what to do. Should he leave? He certainly didn't feel like walking a lap of the field now, but something inside told him to walk over instead.

'You're a good goal kicker,' he said. They were the only words he could think of that he knew wouldn't make Daniel angry.

'Thanks,' Daniel replied. 'You're a great runner.'

Sione was stunned. He didn't know what he was expecting, but that definitely wasn't it. 'Thanks.'

They both stood there saying nothing for a long time, until Sione surprised himself by being the one who broke the silence. 'When did you start playing rugby?' he asked.

'When I was six, I think,' Daniel answered. 'We started doing it for PE at school, and when I was a bit older I started playing on a real team.'

'Hey, same as me!' Sione said, perking up. 'Dad took me to the local club when I was six. It wasn't proper rugby – it was some kid's version. But, yeah, been playing ever since.'

'That was at the Tigers?'

Sione shook his head. 'We move, like, every year. That was in a whole other town.'

'Oh,' Daniel said, kicking the grass. 'It's weird. If I didn't go to Barton, we'd probably be playing on the same team, I reckon.'

'Maybe.'

'My dad loves rugby. He's wanted me to play ever since I was born, so I would be playing somewhere, I know it.'

'That's like my dad, too,' Sione said, breaking into a smile. 'If it wasn't for him I wouldn't be playing.'

'Maybe I could come watch the Tigers play one day,' Daniel said.

'Yeah, and I could come see you play too.'

A heavy footfall sounded behind them, and they both turned to see Izzy approaching.

'Hey, guys,' he said, 'want to practise some passing before we have to go?'

'Sure!' the boys said in unison.

They stood in a triangle, passing the ball around, first in one direction and then the other. In the trees behind them, kookaburras called and a plane flew by overhead.

DANIEL

Daniel climbed onto the bus and sat beside Sione. 'This will be easier than talking across the aisle,' he said casually.

Sione nodded, a smile curling his lips.

Daniel looked past Sione and out the window as the bus rumbled along the driveway. The trees and buildings of the conference centre that had become so familiar so quickly were soon left behind. He was surprised to find he was sad to leave. The thing was, he realised, this weekend hadn't just been about rugby. He'd met his new team, he'd had fun on the field for the first time in ages and he'd made new friends.

In a few hours, the team would be on their way to the Gold Coast to continue their training and play exhibition games against local teams. It would provide them with a much tougher opposition than playing intra-team games could ever produce. *Plus*, Daniel told himself, *Izzy probably thinks going on a trip will help us to bond as a team*. He remembered what Jake had said about a hundred times that morning – 'As long as

I get to go to a theme park, I'll be happy' —
and chuckled.

Sione and Daniel talked about everything
but rugby on the way to the airport. They
told each other about where they lived, what
their school uniforms looked like, and their
families. They even discovered they had one
major thing in common, but it was something
neither boy wanted to talk about just yet.

When the bus pulled up at the airport,
everyone cheered and clamoured to get off
the bus. All except for Sione, who slunk down
low in his seat.

'What's wrong?' Daniel asked. 'Don't like
flying?'

Sione shook his head. 'I haven't been on a
plane since I was a baby.'

Daniel was slightly taken aback, but he tried to not let his surprise show. 'Don't worry, it's nothing,' he said. 'You'll probably get your own TV. They give you food and we'll go up even higher than the clouds – it's heaps of fun!'

'Really?' Sione said, sounding unconvinced.

'Yeah. Come on, I'll sit next to you on the plane, too.'

'Okay,' Sione replied, standing up. 'You can have the window seat this time.'

They walked out of the bus together, and Izzy smiled at them as they walked past. Then, all three said thank you and goodbye to their driver and they walked inside the terminal.

'My uncle is an air steward,' Daniel said. 'He's been all over the world millions of times. I think it would be a cool job, but Dad says I won't have much time for a job like that with uni and playing rugby for Australia.' Daniel could see Sione squirm at this and decided to change tack. 'Look, here's where we check in our bags, then we go through the security area over there and then wait at our gate to board the plane. Maybe we could go and look at the shops and stuff first. It's easy. It's just like a huge train station.'

And it did go easily. They were soon on the plane, waiting for lift-off.

'It's very noisy in here,' Sione observed, looking around the cabin.

Daniel nodded. 'It's normal. You'll get used to it – it's the engines or the air systems or something. Try to block it out. That's a trick we'll have to get used to if we are going to be playing lots of games in front of huge, unfriendly crowds!'

Sione laughed and tried to settle in, exploring the in-flight entertainment options. He watched the flight crew perform the safety instructions as the plane drove around the tarmac and then . . . Wow!

The speed of the plane was tremendous as it shot forwards. The rumbling from the engines and wheels along the tarmac was deafening. Just when Daniel wondered how much more of the runway there could be, the plane became noticeably lighter and the vibrations coming up through the floor disappeared. They were in the air!

Daniel turned to Sione and found that he was smiling so wide that Daniel could have counted all of his teeth.

'Wooooohooooo!' they both cried as the plane climbed higher. This was as good as any theme-park ride!

Izzy's familiar voice filled the air. 'Valley! Valley! Valley!' he chanted.

'Oi! Oi! Oi!' the boys yelled back.

Daniel and Sione turned to each other and grinned. This was it. It was really happening. They were representative rugby players, on their way to unknown adventures with their team.

REALITY CHECK

WRITTEN BY
DAVID HARDING
ILLUSTRATED BY
JAMES FOSDIKE

RANDOM HOUSE AUSTRALIA

SIONE

The ball is taken from underneath the pile of players, then passed out to the fly-half, the centre and on to the wing. Taito's in the clear! He passes one, two, three defenders, cuts back inside and SCORES! Right under the posts! What an amazing effort by the young winger, gaining the Wallabies the lead in the World Cup final! The home crowd is going wild and rightfully so . . .

1

Sione jolted awake, then looked around at his teammates. The boys were laughing and joking as the bus pulled out of Coolangatta Airport and onto the Gold Coast Highway. Sione sat in his usual way, looking out the window, deep in thought. He yawned, then smiled. The flight to Queensland had been short but fantastic. It was the first time he'd been on a plane since he was a baby, and the fact that he was on it as a representative rugby player with his coach – Wallaby Izzy Folau – had only made it better.

Being selected for the Valley rep side had been a bit of a roller-coaster ride for Sione. He had been flattered, but sure he wasn't worthy of his place on the team. Their three-day stay at a conference centre had been so full of ups and downs that, unlike all of his teammates, Sione was secretly hoping they wouldn't have the time to visit one of the Gold Coast's famous theme parks. He didn't think his stomach could take it!

Daniel, the team's fly-half and self-imposed captain, was sitting next to Sione as he talked with Adam and Jake across the aisle. After a rocky beginning, he and Sione had grown something of a friendship between themselves.

'Check it out, everyone!' Izzy called from the front of the bus. He pointed out the right-hand side of the vehicle as a long stretch of sand and sea became visible. The sun, now beginning to sink lower in the sky, projected its golden rays across the shimmering waves.

Sione had been to the beach before but this was amazing. The sand went for miles!

Some of the boys began asking Izzy and the other adults on tour about when they would be going to the beach and the theme parks. Tom and Mary Parker, acting almost as temporary parents for the twenty boys, laughed.

'We'll see!' Mary said mysteriously, and Izzy winked at them.

Before stopping for the night, however, the Valley boys were taken on a detour to the beach at Surfers Paradise. Though it was getting dark, the place was still packed with swimmers, surfers and beachgoers.

Sione looked out at the seemingly limitless black ocean and listened to its waves crashing on the shore. He shivered. The power of the sea was frightening. He watched the lifesavers take down the red-and-yellow flags. Sione had always disliked swimming in the ocean, and found it more unnerving now that the beach was unguarded.

After the boys had their fill of running around on the sand, they were herded back onto the bus. TJ, the team's fullback, had somehow got sand through his hair and was shaking it out all over the place. A few of the boys who had taken off their shoes to run along the shoreline clambered onto the bus barefooted and dripping wet.

Daniel, sitting next to Sione once again, laughed at their plight. 'You should have thought of that before!' he called, as the bus returned to the road, bound for the Paradise Motor Inn.

Sione collected his bags and looked up at the giant neon palm tree, sighing happily. This was it. He wasn't just a rep player anymore – he was on tour. *Interstate!* For better or worse, he was now on the team. He hoped his performances on the field here would be better than back home.

This time, each boy had his own bed. No bunks! After selecting who slept where, Daniel put his suitcase at the end of his bed and declared himself unpacked.

'You still keeping that then?' Jake asked, watching Sione stick up the email Izzy had sent all of them, inviting them to be part of the Valley rep team.

Sione nodded. 'Of course,' he said simply. 'Izzy wrote it.'

'But we *know* Izzy now,' Adam said. 'We can go down a few doors and actually *talk* to him.'

Sione shrugged. It made him feel good just the same. Getting that email was the first time he had ever felt special as a rugby player.

'Forget about it, guys,' Daniel said, his stomach grumbling. 'Anyway, it's dinnertime.'

The four boys ran out of their room and to the dining room that stood at the front of the property. 'I hope it's steak,' Adam said as they walked inside.

Jake raised an eyebrow. 'Are you kidding? Give me pizza any day.'

They quickly chose a table and sat down as the rest of the team filtered through the doors. Waiters were carrying tubs of food and placing them at a buffet counter that ran along the back wall.

'Awesome!' Daniel said, pumping his fist. 'We can pick what we like.'

'Steak!' Adam yelled.

'Pizza!' Jake shouted.

'Careful, Sione,' Daniel said. 'You have to carry your food back to your table, so make sure you don't drop it like you drop rugby balls.'

The others laughed at this, while Sione sank lower in his seat. *Why did Daniel say that? Is he my friend or not?* Sione sat in silence, fuming.

Before he could say anything, Jeremy Fisk, the tour manager, clapped his hands to get everyone's attention. 'I have a few things to go through with you all before we eat,' he said to the crowd of Valley reps.

Daniel groaned and rolled his eyes.

'First, thanks for a great flight – your behaviour was exceptional. I think we'll have a fantastic four days here. Second, tomorrow we'll go to Sunshine High School. They've been nice enough to lend us an oval to train at for the next few days. We'll be playing our first practice match against one of their sides on Wednesday. There'll also be a game against another school on Thursday, and we leave on Friday. Then, it's on to Darwin and finally Sydney for the Championships.'

Hands shot up all over the dining room.

'What about the beach?' one boy asked.

'When do we go to the theme parks?' said another.

Chuckling, Izzy stood up and quieted everyone. 'Don't worry, we'll be going to the beach a few times,' he said with a big smile. 'We'll train and cool down there after our games.'

'And the theme parks?' Daniel reminded him.

'We just aren't here for very long,' Izzy said. 'We have so much to do in so little time –' the sound of the boys sighing filled the room – 'so we can only spare tomorrow afternoon for roller-coasters and dodgem cars!'

Daniel punched the air in celebration as a deafening cheer rose up from the Valley team. Even Sione joined in this time.

DANIEL

Sunshine High had a couple of football fields and the one that had been loaned to Valley was at the back of the school, along its perimeter, with the beach visible in the distance.

No wonder there's so much sand in the grass, Daniel thought, looking down.

He strapped on his headgear and stood with the others along the touchline. Besides games, training was the greatest part of his week back at home, and it wasn't much different on tour. Daniel loved showing off his skills and working on improving his abilities. He enjoyed it so much that, after each training session, he'd start counting down the hours to the next one.

Izzy kicked off the day's session with warm-up drills that were now so familiar to the team that the boys could have done them in their sleep. They had to do various skipping and stretching exercises, moving back and forth between the line and where Izzy stood.

Daniel took each exercise seriously. He wanted to impress Izzy and his teammates.

This youth rep team and the State Championships would not be the pinnacle of Daniel's rugby career – he had much bigger plans – but performing well in front of the selectors at the state comp was important. His dad had constantly reminded him of this before the tour began and his words 'never settle for second best' rang through Daniel's mind during every training session.

There were passing drills, tackling drills as well as scrum and line-out practice. After that, Izzy separated the team into forwards and backs so that each position could concentrate on their own specific needs.

'Daniel,' Izzy said, 'can you look after the backs for a minute while I do some rucking work with the forwards?'

Daniel nodded, beaming with pride. Jake and Adam shared a look and rolled their eyes, knowing they wouldn't hear the end of it that night.

Izzy gave him a thumbs up. 'Simply send them all back towards the tryline while you kick for touch from here. Just make sure you don't let it go into touch so they have to gain possession of the ball before passing it along the back line, okay?'

'Sure,' Daniel said, and Izzy jogged off to the other half of the field with the forwards. 'Gather around, everyone,' Daniel ordered, beckoning for the boys to form a semicircle around him. The backs did so reluctantly. 'Listen up, I'll be your coach for this drill and I only want to explain it once, okay?'

16

Eric, one of the centres, laughed. 'Who are you? Coach of the Wallabies? Don't talk to us like that.'

Daniel shot him a dark look. 'Izzy's asked me to run this, so do as I say.'

'You sound stuck-up,' said Steven, one of the wingers, and everyone laughed. 'Just talk normally.'

'Hey! Listen to me or you're all on the bench tomorrow,' Daniel demanded.

'You can't say that!' Steven said.

'Who do you think you are, anyway?' said another boy.

Eric folded his arms across his chest. 'He only asked you to run this because you're the kicker.'

Izzy looked over to the group of backs and frowned. They hadn't begun their drills yet. 'Daniel, is everything okay there?' he called.

Daniel gulped. 'Yeah, except no one is listening to what I'm trying to tell them.'

Izzy jogged over to investigate the situation and explain the drill to everyone. 'I'll be back in a few minutes to see how you're going,' he said to the group, 'but right now I'm trying to work with the forwards. Daniel's running this until I get back, and I'm more than happy for him to do it.'

'See!' Daniel sneered.

Izzy bent down and whispered in the boy's ear. 'You may find the boys are more receptive if you treat them nicely. Remember – a smile goes a long way.' He smiled wide at the backs to show Daniel what he meant.

'Ow!'

Izzy and the boys turned to see Adam at the bottom of a tackle, holding his leg in pain. The other forwards lifted themselves off him and he rolled about on the grass.

'What happened?' Izzy said, running towards him with all the backs following close behind. Tom and Mary ran in from the touchline with a first-aid kit.

'I don't know,' Jake piped up. 'Adam had the ball and we tackled him and then he screamed.'

'But I asked you guys not to go ahead without me,' Izzy said. 'Adam, are you all right?'

Tom checked Adam's leg. 'I think he's sprained his ankle. We'll take him to the medical centre.'

Izzy nodded while all the boys looked down at their teammate in silence. Mary pulled some icepacks from an esky and expertly taped them to Adam's ankle before he limped from the field, supported on either side by her and Tom.

The boys called out words of comfort and Adam gingerly held up a hand in thanks.

'Well, that's certainly taken the wind out of things, hasn't it?' Izzy said.

Daniel was stunned. Adam was a great hooker who they needed on their team, but more than that, he was a fun guy. Was his tour over? Would he have to go home? All the boys knew that injury was possible, but it wasn't something any of them had ever expected to happen on their tour. Daniel had been so confident only moments before, but now it felt like their team was a puzzle with a big piece missing.

The room was quiet as Jake, Sione and Daniel got ready for their trip to the theme park. What was potentially going to be the highlight of the entire trip now seemed like a waste of time.

'Do you think he'll be okay?' Sione asked for the hundredth time.

Daniel didn't bother to answer, he just shrugged his shoulders and tied his shoelaces. Then there was a knock at the door and Jake went to open it.

'Adam!' he said in surprise.

Adam limped into the room, with the help of two metal crutches. He was still in his training gear, one boot in his hand, his injured foot heavily strapped. 'Hey, guys.'

'Are you okay? How's the leg? Want me to help?' Sione asked.

Daniel laughed. 'If you didn't notice, he's been a little worried about you. Are you going to be okay?'

Adam nodded. 'It's only a sprain. They said I should be walking in a few days, but I won't be in any of the Gold Coast games.'

'So you can play in Darwin?' Jake asked. 'You don't have to go home?'

'No, look! It's better already.' Adam showed that he was able to put a little bit of weight on his injured foot.

'Don't!' Sione yelled. 'You'll make it worse.'

'Can you come to the theme park?' Daniel asked.

Adam shook his head. 'I can't go on the rides or anything, so I might as well stay behind.'

'Just come anyway,' Daniel said. 'We'll walk with you. Even if we have to miss out on some stuff, you're part of the team – you're coming!'

For once, Daniel's forthright attitude was welcomed. Jake and Sione agreed whole-heartedly – they were all in this together and they would stick with Adam, even if it meant a less exciting afternoon for them.

'Besides,' Daniel continued, 'you don't want to miss out on going to a theme park with Izzy Folau, do you?'

Adam got dressed as quickly as he could and the four of them were soon walking to the team's bus at the front of the Paradise Motor Inn. They were the last to get on, and when Adam's face appeared at the front of the bus, all the other Valley players broke into loud applause.

'Three cheers for Adam!' Daniel shouted, and the team obeyed his command.

'HOORAY!'

SIONE

Sione felt a thrill as he walked through the gates of the theme park. He brushed past the crowds, smelled the popcorn and marvelled at the people dressed up as cartoon characters. But as happy as he was, nothing compared to Daniel's excitement. He was so full of beans to be there that he was literally jumping all over the place.

27

After the boys were organised into their groups and a meeting spot was determined, Sione, Adam, Jake, TJ and Izzy followed Daniel to the first destination. Daniel headed straight for the biggest roller-coaster Sione had ever laid eyes on. The rest of the group walked behind him at a slower pace in order to stay with Adam – something that Daniel seemed oblivious to.

'We said we were going to stick with Adam and do things he would be able to do,' Jake said. 'Why are we running to the roller-coasters first?'

Adam shrugged as best as he could while on his crutches.

'This might help Daniel to get it out of his system,' Izzy suggested. 'Then we'll go watch a stunt show or something that we can all enjoy. We're only here for a few hours.'

'Can't we just let Daniel do his own thing and meet up with him later?' TJ said as Daniel called to them to hurry up.

Izzy chuckled and shook his head. 'We should stick together, mate. I can't lose one of the team here – we'd never find them again!'

They soon found themselves standing in front of The Viper, a towering, steel construction. *It looks more like something that has been designed to maim people than entertain them*, Sione thought. He watched a green train zoom up and down at lightning speed. As it looped high in the sky, screams could be heard coming from its carriages. One of the trains pulled to a stop nearby and dozens of people emerged, dizzy and flustered, with their hair in knots.

'I'll stay behind with Adam,' Sione offered, already feeling queasy. 'You guys go.'

'Come on!' Daniel called to them, already in the queue.

'Are you sure?' Izzy asked. 'Please don't wander off, though.'

As a row of carriages roared along the tracks overhead, Sione nodded his head. 'We'll wait on this bench for you.'

Izzy patted Sione on the shoulder as he sat down with Adam to watch the boys have their adventure. Adam was sitting with his injured leg straight out in front of him, his back curved and his face in his hands.

'You all right?' Sione asked.

Adam looked up at him, his eyes red. 'I'm okay to go on it.'

'The signs say you can't go on the rides if you are sick or injured. We can't have your foot getting worse as you thrash around on a roller-coaster.'

Adam grunted. 'I don't even know why I came.'

'To stick together, remember? We're a team.'

The two boys sat in silence for what seemed like forever as they waited for their teammates to return. When they did, there was no missing them. Now, everyone was jumping around, giddy with excitement.

'That was so awesome!' they yelled over and over again, to no one in particular.

Adam and Sione looked up at them and said nothing.

'It really was great,' Izzy agreed. 'Sione, do you want a turn? I'm sure the others won't mind going again.'

'Are you kidding?' Daniel said. 'There's so much more to do – come on!'

He, TJ and Jake raced away, leaving Sione, Adam and Izzy in their dust.

Sione and Adam sat together as the others tried a flume water ride, a crazy octopus contraption that threw its passengers all over the place, another roller-coaster and a ride that was clearly designed just to spin people until they were sick. Izzy came over to chat to the boys between rides and to make sure they were all right, but Daniel and the others were having too much fun to slow down – even for a minute. Sione didn't get it. Why was he the only one who remembered the pact with Adam? He felt so sorry for him and wanted to keep him company, but none of the other boys seemed to care at all.

'This is ridiculous,' Adam said finally, standing up and hobbling towards a food stand.

Sione hesitated, unsure of whether he should join him or wait for the others. 'Hey, where are you going?' he called. When Adam didn't respond, Sione decided to run after him. 'What are you doing?'

'Relax,' Adam replied. 'I feel like an idiot sitting around doing nothing. People keep looking at me and wondering why I'm even here. I'm getting a drink.'

The boys both bought a milkshake and Sione helped Adam by carrying his cup back to the bench for him. 'I'm sorry the others haven't been spending time with you,' Sione said.

Adam shrugged, looking at the ground. 'I can't ask them not to have fun.'

They sat silently for a while, sucking on their straws. 'The milkshake is nice,' Sione said. He cringed inwardly; he never knew what to say in these situations.

'Yeah, almost as good as The Viper, I'm sure,' Adam answered sarcastically.

Sione wanted to tell the other boys off, but he didn't have the guts. He could sense Izzy understood Adam's pain but he was sort of stuck, needing to look after the majority of the group. Soon enough, however, the others returned and Sione was glad to discover he didn't have to be the one to lay down the hard word.

'I'm sitting here bored to death with Sione,' Adam announced. 'You guys said we were a team. Can we do something together now?'

'Well, I need to go to the toilet,' Jake said. 'We could all go do that.'

Adam narrowed his eyes at him. 'Not funny.'

'Look, it's almost three o'clock,' Izzy said, stepping between them. 'That's when the Wild West show is on. Judging from the map, it's not far from here. Why don't we go and see that?'

The boys agreed reluctantly.

'Do we have time for one more ride first?' Daniel asked.

Izzy shook his head and laughed. 'No, mate. I think you've had enough rides to last a lifetime, anyway.'

They got to the arena earlier than most spectators, so the group chose to sit right at the front. They found themselves at the bottom of an amphitheatre, in front of a Wild West scene. The seats for the audience were actually stone steps that went down towards a cluster of wagons and a saloon. 'If we sit at the front,' Daniel had suggested, 'then we won't see the crowd and it will feel more like we are there.'

The rest agreed, but for Adam, hobbling down to the front was a nightmare on his crutches. Izzy and Sione helped him down, walking on either side of him.

'I'm very proud of you both,' Izzy said as they walked. 'You're showing strength during adversity. You've both missed out today but you've done it with a smile.'

Sione saw Adam look down guiltily.

'I'm serious,' Izzy said. 'Other people would have had a tantrum about this but you boys have shown the others what being a team is all about.'

They finally got to the bottom and Izzy helped Adam sit next to Jake. There was no more room on that side, so Izzy and Sione went to sit at the other end of the row, next to Daniel. As they did, the music started, announcing the beginning of the show.

'This had better be good,' Daniel muttered under his breath.

'Sione,' Izzy whispered into his ear, as the first cowboy came out to loud applause, 'I want you to remember what today was like.'

Sione turned to him, confused. 'Huh?'

'Tomorrow afternoon. Remember what it's like to be doing something different, to be out of place, to miss out on what you would rather do.'

'I don't get it. Why?' Sione asked, but his words were drowned out by the noise of guns, horses and cowboys falling from roofs and into hay bales.

SIONE

Sione hurried onto the bus and chose the seat in the back corner. To his surprise, Daniel, possibly out of habit more than choice, decided to collapse in the seat next to him. They rode together in silence, Sione deep in thought and Daniel busy flicking through all the photos on his phone.

Seeing images of Daniel's family and friends made Sione think of home. He was surprised at how little he had actually thought about his family. He messaged them every day but the conversations weren't very long. He smiled, thinking about his little sister, Mele, who was probably in the bath at that moment, crying as their aunty washed her hair. His dad would be dozing on the lounge, watching something rugby-related.

Sione turned away from the brightly lit streets outside his window to peek at Daniel's phone. He had been looking at that one photo for a long time. Sione recognised the boy in the picture as a younger version of Daniel. He was in the lap of a woman with very long hair. She was laughing at the camera.

'Is that your mum?' he asked.

'Yep.'

Sione felt awkward pursuing the conversation but knew it would be just as awkward for it to end there. 'Do you see her much?'

'No, she lives in Perth.'

'Why?'

Daniel sighed. 'She works there. She came from there. She met dad and they got married and moved to where we live. Dad stayed, Mum went back.'

'Oh.' Sione nodded. 'Why?' he wondered aloud.

Daniel put his phone away. 'They got a divorce two years ago.'

Sione rested his head on the back of the seat and looked up at the ceiling. He hated that word. He didn't understand why people would decide to live apart when they had a family together. It felt like the opposite of being on a team.

'Your parents are divorced, too, right?' Daniel asked.

Sione paused before nodding. He looked out the window, blinking back tears. Images of cowboys getting shot and falling from windows cluttered his mind.

The next morning was all sunscreen and board shorts. After breakfast, the boys walked to the local beach for their morning training session. Sione couldn't get over how the beach was just a few blocks down the road. Back home, the closest beach was two train rides and a bus trip away. Kids here seemed to have everything – sunshine, beaches and theme parks. What an awesome life!

While walking to the beach, the boys passed Sunshine High. Sione couldn't help but smile as wide, jealous eyes watched him and the rest of the team walk past with their beach towels and goggles.

When they got to the beach, Mary announced that they would have a bit of free time before Izzy ran them through some drills.

'What? Here on the beach?' Daniel said.

'Yes,' Izzy answered with a grin. 'Here on the beach. You'll see.'

Adam had come too. Tom was going to give him some simple exercises to do in the water as the others trained. His ankle was already looking better than it did yesterday. He still needed the help of the crutches to get to the beach but was able to limp around and wade in the water with the others.

Mary's voice was a constant presence as they goofed around in the surf. 'Stay between the flags!' she yelled at every opportunity. It soon became a joke as other boys began mimicking her voice whenever someone ventured more than a millimetre from the flags' safety zone.

'Stay between the flags! Stay between the flags!' Daniel squealed when Mary went for a short walk along the beach.

'You'll be the death of me, Daniel Masters!' she laughed, and altered the route of her walk, making quick laps between the flags instead of following her original path to the rock pools.

Izzy then organised the team into a game of touch footy.

'I thought you said we would be training,' Jake said, 'not playing.'

Izzy smiled at him. 'Can't they be the same thing?'

But what everyone thought would be a quick, easy game turned into a whole lot of hard work. Running barefoot on the sand was a totally different challenge to playing on grass. Each step was an effort, and Sione found it near impossible to stay at pace. Everyone was moving as if in slow motion.

'It's great exercise for your legs,' Izzy said, after one boy sank into the sand in exasperation. 'If you can run here, imagine how well you'll run on the field!'

Sione watched as Daniel rose to the occasion, darting between players and pulling off fancy passes. Some of the others groaned in annoyance but Sione admitted to himself that he was more than a little jealous. Daniel was someone who played rugby full-on, no matter the situation.

The team also did some running drills but were soon too exhausted to go on. Izzy then led them down the beach for a swim to cool off before heading back to the motel for lunch.

On the way, Daniel pointed to some Sunshine High boys training on the field at the school.

'Look, they're getting ready for us,' he said. 'Fat lot of good that will do.'

Izzy shook his head. The kid sure was competitive. 'Daniel, that's not very polite,' he said.

Daniel shrugged. 'They can't hear. Besides, it's true. We're a rep team!'

The Valley boys stopped to watch Sunshine High play. Sione couldn't help but admit that he didn't see anything extra-special about them, except for the size of some of their forwards. They looked huge, even from a distance.

Sione watched as the goal kicker slotted the ball home from what must have been forty metres out. The boy then went for a run to the opposite tryline and back before setting up his next goal attempt. Now they looked slick. They did the little things, like connecting passes and picking up the ball cleanly.

Daniel continued to rave about how great Valley were all the way to lunch, but Sione wasn't so sure anymore. There was no knowing how good they were until they were tested on the field, and Sunshine High looked like they were going to be Valley's first challenge.

DANIEL

The entire team seemed nervous as they warmed up for the practice match. The Valley boys were keeping one eye on the grass below their feet as they ran through their drills, and one eye on the opposition doing likewise on the other side of the field. Daniel was sure he was the only one fully focused and that bothered him.

'Come on, guys, concentrate!' he cried, after their scrum-half tripped over during the dynamic stretching. 'It isn't that hard to stretch your quads as you move, you know,' he said, earning a dirty look from Harrison in return.

'Okay, Valley, we're about to start,' Izzy called. 'Get your water in.'

Everyone gulped from their water bottles. The day had turned hot, much hotter for a game of rugby than most of them were used to.

'You all look great in your Valley green,' Izzy said approvingly. 'I want you to play your best and make us proud, but –'

'*But?!*' Daniel baulked. *Pep talks should never contain the word 'but'*, he thought.

'But,' Izzy repeated, 'remember that this is still a *practice* match. We are here to improve our skills and the way we work as a team. I'm going to be mixing some things up today, partly to work around Adam's injury and partly to see how we go.

'It's our first game against a real team, and I'm really excited. I still remember the great feeling I got when I first stepped onto the field as a Wallaby. I hope you have a lot of fun out there. If you're on the bench for part of this, don't take that as a knock against your talent. Remember, there are twenty of us and only fifteen spots on the field.'

Daniel listened intently, knowing his position was safe at fly-half.

Izzy went on to announce a few changes to the forward line, which was to be expected with Adam out, but on top of this, Sione was moved to start off the field while TJ was given Sione's position at wing. Daniel thought this was strange as TJ had been looking great as fullback.

The starting fifteen for Valley lined up on the halfway line and shook hands with the Sunshine squad. Each of their players looked at Daniel square in the eyes. Their voices wished him good luck, but their eyes said, 'Because you'll need it'.

It was an intensity that Daniel had rarely seen in a team, but his courage didn't falter. After the toss it was determined that Valley would receive the kick-off and Daniel gathered the team around him for another pep talk.

'This is bad,' said Tezza, one of the flankers. 'We hardly know each other, they've got everything to play for. How good would they feel to take down a rep team!'

'Yeah, look at them,' Jake said. He was one of the few forwards to keep his usual spot at prop. 'You can see steam coming from their nostrils.'

'Hey,' Daniel said, 'let's focus here! They may look intimidating and think they're great, but we'll show them. Remember that you've been chosen for this team for a reason. You're good! We can do this and show them who's on top.'

'Maybe they're just better at rugby here,' Tezza said. 'We're rep players at home, but would we be up here?'

'I think you've been hanging around Sione too much,' Daniel snapped. 'Stop acting defeated before we've played. We can win this, I know it!'

But it soon became very apparent that they couldn't. Within five minutes, Sunshine had forced a turnover, won a scrum and scored a try. Waiting for the conversion kick, Daniel unclipped his headgear in disgust.

'Jeremy, what was that?' he shouted. 'A knock-on? You weren't under any pressure. What a waste!'

When Valley finally did get the ball, Daniel passed it to Tezza expertly, only to have him fumble it a couple of times before getting crushed by a thumping tackle that caused them to lose ground and forced Daniel to kick the ball upfield. There were dropped passes, more knock-ons and missed tackles. Soon, the score was five tries to nothing.

'Valley! Get the little things right – we're making too many mistakes. We're better than this,' Daniel yelled.

In one ruck, a Sunshine forward looked straight at Daniel and grunted, 'And you guys are a rep team?'

By the half-time whistle, Daniel was fuming. 'Basics, basics, basics!' he yelled as the teams walked off, partly so the opposition would hear him and know that at least *he* wasn't to blame for their poor showing. 'Catch passes! Make your tackles!'

'Shut up!' Jake shouted. 'Who do you think you are, anyway? Who said you were the captain?'

Daniel stood there, speechless. Why was he the only one trying to take some responsibility and leadership of the group? Didn't anyone care how well they played?

Izzy ran onto the field. 'Daniel!' he called.

Daniel threw up his arms. He couldn't believe Izzy was going to side with the other boys *again*.

'Listen, you're right,' Izzy said. 'We do need to concentrate on the basics, but yelling at people doesn't help them to listen to the message any better.'

The other boys walked off the field, casting glances their way.

'But how can you make them listen if you don't tell them?' Daniel asked.

'Show them! Remember that this is just a practice match to get us ready for the Championships. We are here to push ourselves and practise our plays. It's about getting used to playing against strangers.'

Daniel didn't agree but he had no other option than to do as he was told. He joined up with his team as they gobbled orange quarters on the touchline. No one said anything, except for Izzy.

'I'm making a change – Sione is coming on now but not as wing. Kane, you come off for a spell. Sione will be in Adam's place at hooker for the second half.'

'What?!' Daniel shrieked. Sione was a back, not a forward. He had probably never been in a scrum in his life. This was crazy talk!

Daniel ran up to Izzy to complain, only to find that Sione had beaten him to it.

SIONE

Jake and Benny, the two prop-forwards, stood on either side of Sione and put their arms around his shoulders. Then Sione did the same to them. He jiggled his arms a bit to ensure they were firmly linked together.

The first few minutes of the second half had passed easily enough. Sione had helped to make a few tackles and, thankfully, the opposition hadn't scored. But now things had taken a dramatic turn for Sione. He had watched enough scrums in his life to have the basic idea of what to do, but it felt strange to be so close to his teammates. As a winger, he'd never done anything like this. The scrum always looked weird from out near the sideline. *It's like a gigantic tarantula*, Sione thought. *Who invented doing this crazy thing, anyway?*

The teacher who was acting as referee looked them over as the second row grabbed Sione's shorts. They were getting ready to push from behind.

'Set!' bellowed the ref, and the opposing team's front row lunged forward, hurtling themselves into Sione and his team like a thunderclap.

But Sione wasn't ready. He hadn't leant forward to meet them. The other team had somehow slotted their heads and shoulders on either side of Sione's body and were pushing him back, hard. Sione was pinned, standing up tall with nothing to push against.

'Put your head down, Sione!' Izzy's voice echoed from the sideline. 'You've got to put your head down!'

He didn't sound cross, but that didn't stop Sione from feeling embarrassed.

'I can't,' Sione squeaked, after another big push from the Sunshine boys crushed the wind out of him. He could see the referee looking at him, his eyebrows down so low they were almost tickling his nose. The referee's face seemed to be asking, 'Don't you know what you're doing?'

Sione wanted to shout, 'It's not my fault. I've never played hooker before!' but he held back the urge.

The ref blew his whistle and everyone stopped. The forwards all groaned and stood up, knowing that the energy they'd expended had all been a waste. Sione watched the giant tarantula dissolve around him.

'It was supposed to be a scrum, not a hug,' the opposing hooker muttered, turning away.

Sione blushed when he saw Harrison standing next to the ref with the ball still in one hand. He hadn't even had a chance to feed the ball into the scrum.

'Okay, we're going to try that again,' the ref said. He looked straight at Sione. 'Are you ready, son?'

Sione nodded as his front-row partners linked their bodies with his again.

'Get ready, lower yourself now!' Izzy called from the sideline.

The opposing hooker, who was facing Sione, grinned. 'He's right. You better get ready for it.'

Sione took a deep breath and bent his knees, leaning against Jake and Benny. The second row engaged behind him and he was soon ducking his head and pushing against the three giant Sunshine forwards.

Being inside the scrum was like being in a cramped tent. A sort of room was created beneath him and the others, their bodies acting like a roof. There was shouting and grunting as the Sunshine boys started pushing Sione and the other Valley boys backward. As the ball was fed to Sione's feet, football boots from all directions started kicking and scraping his shins, trying to get some purchase on the ball. This was nothing like the scrum machine at training. *It* never snarled or kicked back!

As the foot fight escalated, Sione tried to push back against the other team, but the frantic activity at grass level was too much. The Sunshine team pushed themselves over the ball until it spat out the back of their end of the scrum. Sione could see glimpses of the ball then being passed between a couple of their players before it was kicked high, over the remains of the scrum, and behind him.

It was a great kick for touch – there would now be a line-out no more than thirty metres from Sunshine's tryline. The ref blew his whistle and all the players started jogging up to where the line-out would be formed. Sione passed by Izzy and the reserves and was motioned to come off. Zach ran onto the field to take his place. Sione stepped over the sideline and sighed, much louder than he was planning to.

Izzy patted his back. 'Don't worry, you'll be going back out there.'

'No,' Sione said miserably, 'I'm not good enough. I don't want to do that again.'

'There's no way you are going to become the great player that you could be with that attitude,' Izzy replied. 'You *are* good enough.'

Sione sat cross-legged on the grass, his head in his hands. He knew Izzy was trying to cheer him up but he just wanted to be left alone. He thought about Aunty, Dad and Mele back home. He wondered what they were doing. A tear threatened to fall from the corner of his eye but Sione fought it back.

Izzy squatted down next to Sione as the ref's whistle blew and the grunts and groans recommenced further down the field. 'You have what it takes; you could be something amazing if you keep trying.'

Sione lifted his head but still couldn't look Izzy in the eyes.

'When I was calling out for you to keep your head down I wasn't just talking about the scrum. Through every game, and outside of the game too, if you focus, push and do your best, I know you can be great.'

Sione's mouth wanted to smile, just a little, but he fought the urge. 'Maybe, but I'm never going to be great as a hooker. Put me back on as a winger,' he replied, astonishing himself as the words came out of his mouth.

Izzy stood up again. 'We'll see. I'm going to try out TJ on the wing first.'

The sound of boys cheering and clapping rose up from the other end of the field, and Sione knew it meant that Sunshine High had scored the first try of the half.

'Look,' Izzy said, 'whether or not you become a famous hooker, that's where I need you to play now. Put your head down, do your best and help your team – that's what it's all about, not how you look to the crowds.'

Sione exhaled loudly.

'When I began to learn how to play Australian football, I not only had to get used to a new position but an entirely new sport,' Izzy continued. 'It was hard – really hard. But I stuck it out. I tried, I learnt, I had fun even though it felt strange at first. And then I did it all over again when I came to rugby union.'

Izzy left Sione to process his words. He clapped as he jogged over to the Valley players on the field, yelling words of encouragement to them as the school's goal kicker missed the conversion.

Sione looked up. He knew Izzy was right, though he was still angry that he'd been moved. He just had to see it as an opportunity now. If he could become a great hooker . . . well, nothing would be too hard for him.

Izzy returned to the bench and told Sione he was going back on as hooker. 'Basics – don't forget your basics. Strong legs, strong arms, run hard, push!'

Sione nodded and stood up tall, pushing out his chest as the whistle blew and the referee called them all back to restart the game. *This is it*, Sione thought. *I'm going to play my best for Izzy and the others.*

Daniel set the ball on the halfway line and, once both sides were ready, he kicked it to restart the game. It went much further and higher into the air than Sione was expecting, but he thundered after it anyway. Sione, the tall, fast winger, was now a charging rhino of a front-row forward, steaming towards the far-right corner of the field, where the ball was about to drop into the arms of the opposing fullback.

Just as he was about to make the catch, the fullback caught sight of Sione coming at him and did a double take. Sione had got there way faster than any of the other hookers. Caught off-guard, the fullback fumbled the ball. He dropped it behind him as he grabbed at the air, trying to take control of it.

Sione was exhausted but exhilarated. He was giving it his all and it felt good. When the fullback turned and dived on top of the dropped ball in desperation, Sione gladly tumbled on top of him, a split second before four other Valley players did the same.

'Yeah, Sione! Brilliant stuff!' Izzy called.

The ref's whistle blew and the rumbling jumble of kids' legs and arms suddenly stopped struggling as, one by one, all the players climbed off Sione and the fullback.

Daniel patted him on the back as he stood up. 'That was awesome! Now it's scrum time.'

Sione gulped. He found Jake and Benny and the three of them got ready.

'Oh, it's you again.' The Sunshine High hooker smiled. 'The other guy was much better.'

Sione ignored him, and when the two packs collided, he made sure to keep his head down and push as hard as he could. He felt the other forwards behind him, and instead of being intimidated by their pushing, he tried to use it to his advantage.

But they still weren't strong enough. As the scrum started to move the Valley players backwards once again, the ball was fed into its heart. Sione tried using his foot like a hook to scoop the ball behind him, and before he knew it he heard Harrison calling, 'It's out! It's out!' Quickly, he removed himself from the scrum. They were only five metres out!

Eric received a pass and got a metre closer to scoring before getting tackled. Sione's instinct was to snatch the ball from Eric's hands and run to the tryline, but he knew that wasn't the best option. Eric turned on the ground, placed the ball behind him and Sione came in to ruck, pushing the Sunshine players back before they could steal the ball. Benny and Jake joined in and they formed a bubble around Eric and the ball.

Daniel threw his hands between the legs and bodies, plucked the ball free and passed it to the next back further down the line. The ball kept moving, stretching the school's defence along the tryline. TJ caught a pass, found a gap and sprawled himself along the ground. He had scored!

Sione jumped into the air, cheering from the other side of the goalposts. They had finally worked as a team – like a well-oiled machine – and it had been awesome.

TJ was getting hugs and high fives. The day before it would have been Sione on the wing, scoring the try. But deep down he knew that without his work in the scrum and the ruck, the try wouldn't have happened at all. Sione remembered Izzy's words from that night on their training camp at the conference centre back home: 'Only one or two players get shown on the video highlights, but none of that great stuff happens without the whole team working together.'

The team ran back to the line for Daniel's conversion kick, while Izzy continued to call out from the touchline, his fists pumping. 'That's it! We did it together!' They were losing badly on the scoreboard but it didn't matter.

As the sun shone brightly across the ground, Sione shielded his eyes and smiled while he ran.

DANIEL

After the match, in which Valley suffered a devastating loss, Daniel wasn't ready to stop and rest just yet. He couldn't get past the fact that he had missed two goals, even though kicking them wouldn't have got Valley anywhere close to Sunshine's score. Those extra points might have mattered in a different match and he didn't want to miss them again.

Daniel was used to being a reliable goal kicker. His schoolmates back home always expected him to make every conversion and penalty, and he wanted the Valley boys to be the same. He slotted his first practice kick right between the goalposts.

Mary's words from the day before echoed in Daniel's mind: 'Stay between the flags!'

His next kick went between the posts as well. The third was a goal but it didn't bisect the posts exactly, so Daniel decided to do that one twice more.

Meanwhile, the rest of the team were packed and ready to leave. 'Come on, Daniel,' Jake called. 'Let's get out of here!'

But Daniel pretended not to hear. This was important. He didn't want to be the reason for losing a game. He wanted to be the reason for *winning* games.

'Stay between the flags . . . Stay between the flags . . .' he repeated to himself.

Izzy jogged up to Daniel after a kick for goal. 'I'm so proud of you,' he said, smiling widely.

Daniel looked up at him in surprise. 'But I missed twice,' he said.

Izzy shrugged. 'Yeah, but look at you now. You're here, straight after the game, working hard to get your basics right. You recognised something you needed to work on without your coach telling you, and here you are practising to make it better.'

Daniel smiled, realising Izzy was right. He was proud of himself, too. 'Just one more?' he said. 'It's a tough shot and I want to get it between the posts.'

Izzy nodded and stepped back.

Daniel ran up to the ball and slotted it home, as if it were the easiest thing in the world. Izzy and the other boys standing by the gate clapped.

'See?' Daniel said. 'Right between the flags, just like at the beach.'

Izzy chuckled. 'Speaking of which, that's where we're going now,' he said, pointing at the others. 'It's time for a recovery swim. You've got to look after your body as well as your goal kicking.'

Reluctantly, Daniel gathered his things

and began to follow slowly behind the team, with Izzy walking beside him.

'You're showing great captaincy potential,' Izzy said as they walked.

Daniel gasped. 'Really? But you were telling me off before for being too bossy.'

'Well, there's a way to speak to players that you still have to learn,' Izzy said, 'but the boys know you care.'

'I want to win.'

'Yes, but you also want to be your best. You want the whole team to play to their potential. Trust me, not all players think like that.'

Daniel was shocked. He assumed all players wanted their teams to do well.

'Captains have a responsibility to look after their teammates as well as themselves.

Most players find looking after themselves is enough work. You seem happy to push and encourage others, not just yourself. Most of all, you are showing the other boys the meaning of dedication and hard work. You put more time into training than any of them. You study the game. You lead by example – by what you do, not just what you say.'

Daniel hadn't expected Izzy to say anything like this to him. He suddenly felt very proud of himself. 'It's like you,' he said.

'What is?'

'You lead by example, too.'

Izzy smiled. 'We better hurry, or we'll be late for the beach. Bet you can't beat me there!'

With that, the two of them raced off after the rest of the team.

By the time the team got to the beach, the water was freezing. The boys lined up along the shore, unwilling to dive in.

'Come on, don't be shy,' Izzy coaxed them. 'Cold water is good for your muscles after a hard work-out!'

Taking a deep breath, Daniel decided to lead by example. He dashed into the ocean, shivering, until it was up to his waist, then began running through the water, just as Izzy had demonstrated. Soon, the whole team was doing the same, most of them squealing about how cold it was.

They jogged through the waves, pushing their legs against the water's strength. It was hard work, but Izzy was right – it felt good. After two laps either way, the jogging exercise devolved into a splashing game, with laughter coming from all sides.

Izzy then led the boys out of the water and onto the sand for a long stretching session. Usually, stretches were something the boys wanted to rush through. Today, however, exhausted and enjoying the beach, all of them took their time, ensuring their legs, arms and glutes were loosened. Daniel found it relaxing, stretching as waves crashed on the shore twenty metres away.

Before long, a frisbee was brought out and the boys started throwing, catching and falling all over it.

'Stay between the flags,' Mary shouted, more as a joke this time than for safety.

Laughing, Daniel threw a zipping pass across the beach and noticed that Adam was sitting by himself high on a sandhill. He excused himself from the game and jogged up to Adam, his wet feet making squishing sounds as he ran along sand.

'Hey!' he called. 'How's your ankle?'

Adam shrugged. He had hobbled about in the water with the others and had done almost all of the stretches, but he'd had to sit out of the game of frisbee.

'You'll be right in a couple of days,' Daniel said reassuringly.

Adam looked up at him. 'I know. I just hate missing out.'

'Just follow Izzy's advice and you'll get better fast.'

Adam smiled. Daniel was the last person he'd have expected to take time out to comfort him. 'Thanks,' he said.

There was an awkward pause before Daniel nodded and rejoined the game. He could see that this was the start of something new for him as a player, because now he knew it for sure – he was going to be captain of the Wallabies one day.

DANIEL

The next morning saw Daniel and the others doing some light training on the school oval. Despite it being the site of their first match and first defeat as a team, there was no sign of bitterness as the boys ran, passed the ball and tackled. It was as if the previous day's loss had only encouraged them to improve and learn to work better as a team.

'We're returning to basics today,' Izzy announced to the Valley boys. 'The way you will impress me today is by catching the ball, not sidestepping an opponent or trying a backhand pass.'

Daniel usually hated training sessions like this. The drills they were doing reminded him of the boring sessions at the start of every season, where the coach is just interested in seeing what each player can do. Daniel saw himself as match-ready from day one. But, somehow, yesterday's game had changed this. It had made him realise that staying at the top requires just as much hard work as getting there.

First, Izzy divided the boys into four groups. They stood in single file facing each other, as if turned inward from the four points of a square. Two of the boys at the front of their lines were given balls and directed to run into the centre of the square. Once there, they were to pass their ball to the front boy on the line to their right, avoid the oncoming player as the opposite line did the same thing. Then the passer had to run to the back of the line across from them. It was something Daniel had done many times, but as he watched Sione drop the first pass of the drill, Daniel wondered if Sione had.

Wake up, Sione! Get it together! he thought, swallowing the urge to yell it. He took a deep breath and remembered what Izzy had said to him yesterday. 'Don't worry, just get the next one!' he shouted.

Sione almost did a double take in shock. He took a second to recover, then smiled and nodded at Daniel.

At the end of training, Izzy sat the twenty boys down and congratulated them on bouncing back so quickly from yesterday's disappointment.

'Well done,' he said. 'A big defeat often leads to a depressing change room and another loss the next week, but I think you guys have shown enough dedication to improve this morning that I am sure we will play better this afternoon.'

Daniel's eyebrows rose. He'd forgotten they had another practice match today. 'Who are we playing, again?' he asked.

'Maxfield,' Izzy answered. 'They'll be here to play us at two.'

'Are they any good?' Harrison asked.

'Honestly, I don't know.' Izzy laughed. 'Remember, the score doesn't count. This is about improving and practising as a team.'

'And enjoying our holiday,' Jake said. 'Speaking of which, when are we going back to the beach?'

Back at the motel, Daniel walked out of the bathroom to find Sione lying on his bed and staring at the ceiling.

'Worried about the game?' Daniel asked. 'You'll be fine. You did well today.'

Sione shook his head. 'Izzy said I'm back on the wing.'

'Cool!' Daniel exclaimed, instantly realising how harsh that sounded. 'I mean, not that you were bad at hooker or anything.'

Sione sighed. 'Remember what I said about my mum?'

'That your parents are divorced?'

'Yeah.'

'Sure,' Daniel said.

Sione sat up. 'Well . . . they're not really divorced.'

Daniel's stomach twisted. He wasn't sure if he wanted to hear what Sione had to say.

'Mum left.' Sione looked down guiltily.

'What do you mean?'

'One day I woke up and she wasn't there. Never seen her since.'

Daniel was stunned. 'Why?'

Sione wiped his eyes and stood up. 'Dunno,' he said, walking out of the room.

Daniel's shoulders fell. He wished he could have said something comforting but he didn't know what to say. Being a captain and supporting your players both on and off the field was proving to be more difficult than he'd first thought.

SIONE

Sione rushed from the room, overwhelmed with embarrassment. Why had he thought it was a good idea to tell Daniel? He didn't seem to care at all. But Sione had to admit that it felt like a weight had been lifted off his shoulders. He hadn't told anyone about his mum – ever. No one on the Tigers knew, and neither did anyone at school. He didn't even talk about his mum with his dad because he knew it upset him so much, and Mele was too young to understand. But it was constantly on Sione's mind. It was why his aunty had come to live with them, after all.

Sione hoped Daniel wouldn't go around telling everyone else on the team about it. He still couldn't figure Daniel out. He was mean and self-centred one minute, then a great friend the next. Sione knew the better times with Daniel were starting to outnumber the bad times, but still . . . At least he wasn't a liar anymore. It felt right to have finally told Daniel the truth.

As Sione and his teammates stretched for the game against Maxfield, he felt anxious.

Daniel and some of the others were carrying on in their usual way, geeing themselves up for the match. Sione, as always, prepared in silence. He closed his eyes as he stretched, praying that he didn't drop another pass or mess up another scrum.

Surprisingly, Adam sat down next to him to join in the stretching. Adam was now able to walk without crutches but still wasn't ready for a game, so he'd been given the job of waterboy for the afternoon. Sione was pleased, both for Adam and for the fact that it was a scorching-hot day and they had someone to deliver refreshment when it was needed. It was so hot that, for once, Sione wished he was mucking around on the beach instead of playing rugby in the sun.

The Maxfield boys lined up in their red-and-orange stripes on the halfway line to shake hands with Valley. Sione always hated this part of the match. He didn't like shaking hands to begin with, but on top of this, opposing players would sometimes take the opportunity to give you a dirty look or squeeze your hand that little bit too hard.

Sione followed Daniel down the line, his eyes down and his handshakes soft. The match began and Sione had little to do early on. He took two passes well but couldn't shake off the defenders. However, after he landed a tackle on his opposing winger that earned a clap from Izzy on the bench, Sione started to have fun. He was doing what he was used to, in his usual position. No one was expecting him to be a hero, or needing him to be one, and he was doing his bit to help out the team.

Then the unthinkable happened. Sean, playing in Adam's spot at hooker, tripped in a ruck. A football boot came out of nowhere and kicked him in the head. He seemed fine but Tom and Mary Parker were soon ushering him off the field for a proper check-up. Sione could see Izzy's eyes scanning the field. He was looking for someone. *No*, Sione prayed, *please don't move me.*

Their eyes met, and Izzy called to him. 'Sione! You're in the scrum. TJ's coming on to replace you.'

Hooker again? Sione's mind screamed. *This is the worst!*

He trudged across to the middle of the field. The Maxfield front row looked him up and down but said nothing. Jake and Benny both put their arms around his shoulders, and Sione awaited the command to form the scrum.

'Set!' yelled the ref.

Now Sione had a better understanding of what to do, and when his head slotted between the shoulders of his opposition, like an upside-down cradle, he was amazed for the first time at how simple and special the scrum was. No other sport had anything quite like it. He pushed as hard as he could against the Maxfield forwards, his confidence boosted by the strength of his teammates pushing behind him.

The ball was fed, possession was won by Valley and soon Sione was making tackle after tackle. Slowly but surely, Valley managed to push closer to their scoring end. After gathering the ball from a tackle, Harrison passed to Daniel, who made a perfect dummy before running through a gap in the defence. He was dragged down only a metre from the tryline, but managed to slip a pass backwards to Sione, who had been following him closely.

The ball landed in Sione's hands with a couple of Maxfield players directly in front of him. He could see the line. Instinctively, he rose up on his legs to jump over the tackling arms that had risen to block his way, but in a split second he changed his mind. He went in low, below the tacklers' arms, diving beneath them and across the line for five. The red-and-orange Maxfield shirts were a blur on either side of him as Sione landed.

His teammates ran over, cheering. He had propelled Valley in front with a tremendous two seconds that capped off all the work the team had put in to get themselves into the position to score. Sione grinned, his spirits soaring even higher as Daniel easily kicked the conversion.

Play recommenced and Sione flung himself into his role as hooker with gusto, tackling and running hard. He wasn't missing the wing at all.

Towards the end of the game, Sione was swapped back to wing for a much-earned rest. He was surprised to find himself feeling disappointed about the change, but consoled himself that at least he wasn't being taken off. Izzy clearly trusted him to play full games for the team and that seemed even more important than scoring tries.

The full-time whistle blew just as a penalty was awarded. Daniel lined up for a shot at goal, and as he stared down the goalposts, the Valley boys began to chant.

'Stay between the flags! Stay between the flags!' they shouted.

When Daniel kicked the ball high and true, the team didn't just cheer, they laughed and clapped and celebrated. They had won their first game.

DANIEL

'Valley! Three cheers for Maxfield!' Daniel yelled. 'Hip hip!'

'Hooray!' his teammates called.

The Maxfield boys stood in silence, clearly stunned by the gesture, until one of their players returned the favour by starting a cheer in Valley's honour.

'That was awesome, Daniel,' Izzy said, as they gathered to cool down and rehydrate. 'We might even make it a tradition after every game, hey?'

Daniel grinned, chuffed. 'Sure!'

'Well done, everyone,' Izzy said to the boys. 'That was a fantastic display of smooth rugby, and a terrific win.'

'Yeah! The other team didn't score a single point!' Tom added.

Daniel smiled, proud of their work as a team. It was a great achievement so soon after a loss. They had managed to bounce back and play well.

They made their way to the beach for one final recovery swim. Today, the cold dip was enjoyed by all. Nothing – not even the chilly water – could dampen their spirits.

After the swim, Daniel approached Izzy. 'Can I lead the team in the stretching?' he asked tentatively.

Izzy broke into that familiar wide smile, pleased at Daniel's initiative. 'Sure! Go right ahead.'

Daniel ran off and ushered the team into a semicircle in front of him and then demonstrated the first stretch. Even Izzy joined in.

'Yes, sir, captain, sir!' Jake yelled, saluting him, and everyone laughed.

But no one told Daniel to stop or complained that he was being bossy. With each stretch, Daniel gave words of advice or encouragement.

After the cool-down exercises, the boys were relaxed and happy. They packed up their belongings, shaking the sand out of their towels and T-shirts. The walk back to the motel was full of laughter and joking around. Daniel, seeing that Sione was walking by himself near the back of the group, excused himself from the conversation he was having with Jake.

'Great stuff today,' he said cheerfully, appearing at Sione's side.

The boy shrugged. 'I dunno.'

'You were awesome,' Daniel insisted. 'I bet your mum would have been proud to see you play today.'

Sione froze, his hands curling into fists. 'Why did you say *that*?' he hissed.

'W-What do you mean?' Daniel stammered.

Sione's eyes pierced Daniel's. 'Why did you say that? Are you making fun of me?'

'No! Of course not. I just . . .' Daniel faltered. He'd thought it would have been a nice thing to say, but he had clearly made a mistake.

'Why did you say that?' Sione repeated.

Daniel swallowed. He looked up the street. The other boys were now turning into the motel's driveway, oblivious to what was happening behind them. Daniel turned back to look at Sione.

'I'm sorry,' he said eventually. 'I shouldn't have mentioned your mum. I just thought it would cheer you up to know that you played really well today and I thought it would be nice to think of your mum wishing she could be here to watch you.'

Sione glared at Daniel for what seemed like hours. At last, his breathing slowed and he resumed his familiar pose of looking away and down at his feet. 'Sorry, I . . . No one else knows about her, okay?' he said quietly. 'I don't want the others to know.'

Daniel nodded. 'I promise I won't tell anyone.'

After that, they walked back to the motel in silence. Sione seemed to be deep in thought, so Daniel left him alone. He wondered what he had said that had been so wrong. When they reached the driveway, Sione stopped and looked up at Daniel.

'If Mum would be so proud of me playing rugby, then wouldn't she be here to see me?' he asked, searching Daniel's face for an answer. He shook his head. 'She doesn't care. She left, remember?' Sione turned and walked away, leaving Daniel alone on the footpath.

After dinner Tom and Mary announced that they had a surprise for the team. They led the boys into the conference room and sat them down opposite a projector screen. Daniel gasped excitedly, as did the others, when the video began to play. He had no idea that their matches had been recorded! Seeing himself up on the screen was really strange, mostly because it was so different to how he'd always imagined he looked on the field.

'Do I really look like that when I run?' he asked no one in particular.

The boys stared at the screen, laughing one minute and quiet the next. They watched in silence as the match against Sunshine High unfolded before them. Some boys averted their eyes, wincing, and others groaned audibly.

It really is amazing how hard a team takes a loss, Daniel thought. *I'm not the only one who wished it never happened.*

When the footage of him yelling at the others to lift their game rolled onto the screen, Daniel hunched down in embarrassment. He witnessed the dirty looks the others had given him on the field and was stunned, but he couldn't blame them.

They went on to watch the match against Maxfield, and this time the boys whooped and cheered at their smooth play. Each try was celebrated as if they were watching a grand final.

When the clip finished, Izzy stood up. 'The contrasts are striking,' he began. 'I was going to go through the match with you point by point and indicate all the things that we did better in the second game, but I don't think I need to. You know what we did right. We did our basics so well – we made tackles, we hit passes, we ran hard, we kicked between the flags – we were awake!'

Daniel smiled. The game today had been so much fun.

'When we play to our potential we are an amazing team,' Izzy continued. 'I can't wait to see how you perform in the State Championships. But, before I get ahead of myself, we have our stint in the Northern Territory to look forward to.'

Tomorrow, the team was going on a plane to the Northern Territory, and Daniel couldn't wait. The Gold Coast had been great, but he had never been to the Top End before. He wondered if they would see any crocodiles. He hoped so, but it seemed unbelievable that this trip could get any better!

SIONE

Sione opened his eyes and yawned. Waking up hadn't felt this sweet in a long time. The team had really bonded over their experiences on the Gold Coast – first from their the shock loss, and then from their comeback win. Last night had been awesome fun, filled with laughter and jokes. Whenever his mind had drifted back to the incident with Daniel, he'd pushed the thought as far away as he could. He wanted to apologise to Daniel, but that would mean unfurling the ball again, so he dismissed that idea.

Sione sat up and stretched. On the wall next to him was the printout of the email that Izzy had written to him, welcoming him to the rep team. He had continued to keep it next to him during their stay, stuck to the wall so he could read it every morning and night. It helped him to remember that he deserved to be on the Valley team, that this was the right place to be.

He quickly got out of bed and splashed cold water on his face, then put on his training gear so quietly that the other boys didn't so much as rustle in their beds. He shoved his room key in his pocket and jogged outside to the back of the motel, where there was a small patch of grass and a playground. From there, he watched Izzy perform his stretches. Without a word, Sione joined in, taking Izzy's lead.

'How about a jog?' Izzy suggested after a while. He pointed to a route that led around the car park and the pool. 'We could run around there, do some sprints on the grass and then tackle the obstacle course?'

Sione nodded, smiling. This had become the best part of his day by a mile. It was something none of his teammates knew anything about – it was just between him and Izzy Folau, the great Wallabies fullback. What a treat it was, to keep fit and bond silently with Izzy each day.

As they jogged, Sione thought about his life just a week before. Izzy had been an idol from afar, an image on his TV screen or the poster in his bedroom, not an actual, live person who he knew and talked to. Even when he had first stumbled upon Izzy's early-morning training sessions at the training camp back home, Sione had felt shy and unworthy to be there. But, with Izzy's encouragement and support, he now felt confident and at ease during these sessions. Sione felt lucky to have him as a mentor.

They jogged around the circuit five times before Izzy stopped and headed for the grass to do some sprints. 'Having fun?' he asked with a big smile.

Sione grinned and nodded.

'Whereabouts in Tonga is your family from? Nuku'alofa?'

Sione nodded again. It was difficult to speak while running. 'Dad was born there,' he puffed.

'You ever visited?'

'Once, but I was too young to remember.'

They sprinted back and forth across the grass, Sione pushed himself hard and enjoyed every minute of it. It was almost like the beep test Izzy had given the boys a few days before. Sione wasn't sure how many sets they did, but he was puffing and sweating by the time they stopped and walked up to the playground equipment to begin the fun part of the session – the obstacle course.

Two mornings earlier, Izzy had designed a route through the playground that was a tonne of fun. They swung on the flying fox, charged up a ramp, jumped up some steps, ran around the fort, climbed a ladder, did five pull-ups on a set of bars, slid down the slippery dip, scrambled up the little rock-climbing wall, balanced across the bridge and then hopped down, only to do it five more times.

Sione smiled all the way through, though the pull-ups were always a challenge for him.

'You've already come such a long way as a player since the tour began,' Izzy said as they began their cool-down jog. 'I bet part of that has to do with your focus on exercising and eating right. You must be one of the fittest on the team.'

Sione shrugged. 'I just want to be the best player I can be.'

'I'm proud of you,' Izzy said. 'I'm proud of the whole team. You're a bunch of hard-working boys!'

As they sat and stretched in the grass, Sione noticed sand strewn among the green spikes, blown in from the beach. He lay back onto the grass, listening to his breathing and the sound of waves crashing in the distance. He'd never felt so relaxed and he was sad it was almost time to go.

'Wake up, sleepyhead. We have to get to the airport!'

Sione's eyes snapped open to see Jeremy Fisk standing above him. He was wearing board shorts and a towel was draped around his shoulders. Sea water dripped off his hair and landed on Sione's forehead. Sione squeaked and sat up suddenly.

Izzy and Jeremy laughed. 'See you round the breakfast table!' Jeremy called as he made his way back to the motel.

It was the first time Sione had really interacted with Jeremy all trip. He had always been there in the background, organising the group's movements, but he hardly ever spoke. Sione realised every adult on the tour was soft-spoken like he was. Maybe that's why he was starting to feel so comfortable – he had barely thought about home at all.

'Jeremy's a bit of a joker,' Izzy said. 'He was like that when we were little and played footy together.'

'You guys were on the same team?'

Izzy nodded. 'He doesn't play anymore, but we're lucky to have him on tour. He's a great manager.'

Sione wanted to ask why Jeremy stopped playing, but Izzy was standing up and ready to get changed for breakfast. Instead, he asked a question that he had been dying to ask for a while, and he hoped Izzy would be happy to give him an answer. 'Izzy, do you have a mum?'

Izzy smiled. 'Yes. Do you?'

'Yes and no.'

Izzy looked at Sione in a way that suggested he had an idea of what he was talking about. 'I'm sorry to hear that,' he said after a while. Then he looked at the time on his phone. 'I'm happy to chat about anything you like at any time, but we can't be late for the plane. I'll see you at breakfast, okay?'

Sione nodded.

'You're a good kid,' Izzy added, 'and a great player – I mean that.'

Sione looked down at his feet.

'Trust me,' Izzy said. 'If you keep putting in the effort, you'll see the benefits on the field. But you have to believe in yourself, too. Can you do that?'

Sione thought about it for a moment. Believing in himself seemed like a foreign concept. He shrugged.

'Well, *I* trust in you,' Izzy said with a smile. 'You'll do great things for Valley, and anyone else you play for. I know it.'

Sione walked back to his room to find everyone getting ready for breakfast. Daniel appeared from the bathroom, and their eyes met. Neither of them said anything. Somehow, without a word spoken, all was understood and forgiven.

Sione closed the bathroom door behind him, chuckling at the sound of Jake, Adam and Daniel chanting 'N-T! N-T! N-T!'

DANIEL

Returning to Coolangatta Airport was strange. They had only been there four days earlier, but it felt more like four months ago to Daniel. Spending time away from home with other people had really stretched out his days. Perhaps, he wondered, it was the living out of routine, or maybe it was the emotional highs and lows he had been experiencing.

Sione grew less talkative as they lined up to board the plane. This would be his second flight in a week, so Daniel assumed he was already more at home with the idea of flying. Though Sione remained close to Daniel and sat next to him on the plane, he didn't seem anxious about the flight like he did on their first trip.

This time Sione sat next to the window and Daniel took the aisle seat. It was going to be a much longer flight. Darwin would take over twice as long to get to as the Gold Coast had taken from home. Soon enough, the plane roared to life and lifted the Valley team above the clouds. While the other boys excitedly checked out which movies and games were available, Daniel didn't feel like doing anything more than sitting and thinking, which wasn't like him at all. There was one thing that he couldn't shake from his mind. Since Sione had got upset about his mum, Daniel had felt confused and flustered.

Daniel thought about his own parents' divorce. He knew it had been an upsetting time but he couldn't really remember it. He only thought about his mum occasionally these days and he hadn't been troubled by that fact until now. His dad had taught him to be tough and to not get upset by such things, but now Daniel wondered if he should have been.

Why wasn't he upset about losing his mum the way Sione was? Was it because she lived far away? Was he just more brave? Or was it because he was self-centred and didn't care?

Daniel turned to look at Sione. He didn't really understand him. He was quiet, shy and sometimes Daniel wasn't sure if he even wanted to play rugby or be on a rep team. But the thing that made him jealous of Sione was the fact that he knew how he felt. He had emotions. Sometimes Daniel felt more like a statue than a living, breathing person.

He pulled out his phone and put on his headphones. But Daniel didn't turn any music on – the headphones were merely a cover. Instead, he began to type. His fingers, moving slowly at first, soon began tapping on his phone's screen at a ferocious speed.

Hi Mum. I'm writing to you from a plane flying to Darwin! I'm going as part of the rep-team tour around Australia, then it's on to the State Championships. I hope we see a crocodile!

Dad said he'd tell you that I was going on the trip. I hope he did because it has been lots of fun. I've made heaps of friends. We've just played two games on the Gold Coast and we went to the beach every day. And our coach is Izzy Folau!!! He's cool. He even said he thinks I would be a good captain one day, maybe even for the Wallabies! ☺

Do you remember that day we were on the patio and Dad wanted to take a family photo and he was testing the automatic shutter on the camera and I was sitting in your lap? Just as he took a photo I burped accidentally and you started laughing SOOOOO loud. That was really funny. I still have that photo.

Hopefully you can move back or I could move to Perth. One day I will save up enough money to come visit you. When I'm a famous rugby player I will come every week in the off-season.

'Hey, what are you doing?' Adam asked, popping his head up from the seat in front. 'Writing a book?'

'No,' Daniel answered, locking his screen.

'Well, you're missing out. They have the latest episodes of *Hurricane Fighters* on here.'

'Cool, I'll check it out in a sec.' Daniel returned to his email, and quickly added one more paragraph before saving it and turning off his phone.

He lay back in his seat. He realised he had been missing his mum all along. He hoped she could make it to see him and his team holding the State Championships trophy aloft. It would be the greatest moment he could wish for.

SIONE TAITO

POSITION: Wing

SCHOOL: Valley North

TEAM: The Tigers

LOVES TO: Watch Izzy Folau play on TV

Picked to play for the Valley team on the wing, Sione has many attributes that good wingers need. He is fast, fit and able to find a gap within any line of defence. At first, Sione wasn't sure if playing on a rep team was the right fit for him, but since finding his feet with Valley, he has become more comfortable with his selection.

Soft-spoken Sione does all his 'talking' on the rugby field, where he strives to play with the enthusiasm and happiness of his hero, Izzy Folau. Sione plays for the Tigers in his local competition. There, he has excelled and become what many rugby fans might call a 'try-scoring machine', though those are words he would never use to describe himself.

DANIEL MASTERS

POSITION: Fly-half

SCHOOL: Barton Grammar

TEAM: Barton Grammar

LOVES TO: Kick a match-winning goal

Daniel plays for Valley at the vital position of fly-half. As he directs the back line on the field, he also tries hard to lead by example off the field. Daniel's ultimate dream is to captain Australia at the Rugby World Cup. Sometimes his dedication and desire to win get in the way of having a good time, but with Valley, he is learning to do both.

Daniel is also a terrific goal kicker who is never happier than after kicking one hundred per cent of his attempts in a match. His success comes from the extra hard work he puts in after training and on his days off. If there ever was a boy who loved his rugby, it's Daniel. Possibly the most passionate rugby player in the world after Izzy Folau, Daniel never stops giving his all.

VALLEY TEAM

Name: Daniel Masters

Position: Fly-half

Plays for: Barton Grammar

Known for: His accurate goal kicking

Greatest moment: Leading his team to an undefeated season

Name: Sione 'the Eel' Taito

Position: Wing

Plays for: The Tigers

Known for: Weaving through defenders

Greatest moment: Being selected for the Valley rep team

Name: Theo 'TJ' Jones

Position: Fullback

Plays for: Grantham Boys

Known for: Catching high balls under pressure

Greatest moment: Scoring three tries in a grand final

Name: Steven Hendricks

Position: Wing

Plays for: The Bears

Known for: His courage under pressure

Greatest moment: Scoring a try in his first game

Name: Eric Le

Position: Centre

Plays for: Saxby Prep

Known for: Being selected for Valley in his first year playing rugby

Greatest moment: Scoring a hundred-metre try

Name: Joseph Rosenberg

Position: Centre

Plays for: Saxby Prep

Known for: His ability to set up tries

Greatest moment: Putting five other teammates on the scoreboard in one game

Name: Harrison Gordon

Position: Scrum-half

Plays for: Bunyan Bunyips

Known for: His leadership at the scrum

Greatest moment: Winning his team's Best Player trophy two years in a row

Name: Derek 'the Ringmaster' Ngo

Position: Wing

Plays for: Clifton Grammar

Known for: Running rings around the opposition

Greatest moment: Being promoted from the D Team to the A Team at school within two weeks

Name: Ty Fennelly

Position: Fullback

Plays for: St Francis's

Known for: His long kick returns

Greatest moment: Scoring twenty-five points in one match

Name: Jake Hunter

Position: Prop

Plays for: Queens

Known for: His strong tackling

Greatest moment: Playing every minute of every game last season

Name: Benny Simons

Position: Prop

Plays for: Queens

Known for: Pushing opposition teams back in the scrum

Greatest moment: Being selected for two different rep teams in two different states

Name: Adam El-Attar

Position: Hooker

Plays for: St Christopher's

Known for: His jumping in the line-out

Greatest moment: Making thirty tackles in one game

Name: Tim Broadbent

Position: Second row

Plays for: The Saints

Known for: His goal kicking

Greatest moment: His tackle in extra time that saved his team's season

Name: Patrick Mulholland

Position: Second row

Plays for: The Saints

Known for: Taking on any opponent, no matter how big

Greatest moment: Chasing down an opponent from twenty metres behind, then tackling him into touch

Name: Terry 'Tezza' Williams

Position: Flanker

Plays for: The Bears

Known for: His speed down the blind side

Greatest moment: Scoring a try in every game last season

Name: Zach Smith

Position: Flanker

Plays for: St Francis's

Known for: His ability to play as a forward or back

Greatest moment: Being his team's captain and also its youngest player

Name: Nathan Davidson

Position: Number-eight

Plays for: Clifton Grammar

Known for: His seemingly unlimited energy

Greatest moment: Regularly landing twenty-metre-long passes to teammates

Name: Kane Williams

Position: Utility-forward

Plays for: The Saints

Known for: His accurate kicking for touch

Greatest moment: Playing in every forward position last season

Name: Sean de Groot

Position: Utility-forward

Plays for: Clifton Grammar

Known for: His 'never give up' attitude

Greatest moment: Winning a grand final with an extra-time try

Name: Kian Hardy

Position: Utility-forward

Plays for: Clifton Grammar

Known for: Always walking off the field covered in mud

Greatest moment: He has played for three Premiership-winning teams

ISRAEL FOLAU

NICKNAME: Izzy

BORN: 3 April 1989 in Minto, NSW

HEIGHT: 195 cm

WEIGHT: 103 kg

POSITION: Fullback

TEAM: NSW Waratahs, Australian Wallabies

IZZY'S CAREER

2007/08: NRL Melbourne Storm

2007–2009: Australian Kangaroos

2008–2010: Queensland Maroons

2009/10: NRL Brisbane Broncos

2010: NRL All Stars

2011/2012: AFL Greater Western Sydney Giants

2013–present: NSW Waratahs

2013–present: Australian Wallabies

IZZY'S TRAINING TIPS: PASSING

You may think that passing a ball is as simple as tossing it in the air in the direction of one of your teammates. However, to become a great passer, there is a lot to think about before you let the ball leave your fingers.

As you pass a ball, hold it with both hands. Use your hand furthest away from your target to push the ball, and the other one to guide it. Your hands should end up in the direction of your target after letting go.

A successful rugby pass must be of the correct strength and height and be on target.

TARGET: Remember to look at the player you wish to pass the ball to and swing your arms in their direction. If your pass is not accurate, it may not be caught.

STRENGTH: If your pass is too soft it will not reach your target. Too hard, and it will hit them too vigorously. Practise passing from different distances to learn how hard your passes should be.

HEIGHT: This is similar to your strength. If your pass is too high or too low it will be difficult to catch and may be dropped.

Did you know that waiting to pass can be just as important as passing the ball? Sometimes, players want to get rid of the ball as soon as they gain possession of it, but take that split second before you pass to consider your options. Consider who you are going to pass to and whether they are ready to receive it.

Why not try this training drill to improve your passing strength?

Stand a metre away from your partner. Pass the ball to them, remembering correct positioning and technique. If they catch it at their chest, your partner should pass the ball back to you. Whenever both of you successfully pass and receive the ball, both of you can then take a step back. Now the passing distance is greater. How far can you go?

IZZY'S TRAINING TIPS: THE SCRUM

Every rugby team has eight forwards, which is known as 'the pack'. They are usually the bigger players as they tend to do most of the tackling during a game. The forwards also have two other very important jobs: they help to gain possession of the ball after a restart of play, either from a line-out or a scrum.

Scrums are the perfect example of good teamwork on the field. All eight forwards must work together for a successful scrum.

Have you ever wondered what the jobs of the different forwards in a scrum are?

The Front Row is made up of the two props, and the hooker who stands between them. The hooker's job is to try to win the ball for his team with his feet. The props must support the hooker – or 'prop him up' as he works – all the while, engaging with the opposition's front row.

The Second Row is made up of the two locks. They push the scrum from behind the front row. They provide most of the scrum's power.

The Back Row includes the number-eight and two flankers. The number-eight binds behind the locks and gives weight to the scrum. They help to ensure the ball leaves the scrum cleanly. The flankers only connect to the sides of the scrum very loosely so they can quickly detach from it when they need to. They also help to push the scrum at angles.

Scrums are like nothing else in any sport. Crowds watch with bated breath once the ball is fed into a scrum, hoping that their team will win possession of it once again. However, players can be hurt in a scrum if they do not practise correct body position.

Remember these tips for correct body position in a scrum – you could try this in front of a mirror.

1) Stand shoulder-width apart with your feet pointing straight ahead.

2) Shorten your neck, making sure to keep your head in a neutral position.

3) Bend at the hips, then bend at the knees. This will help you to keep the weight off your heels. Your chest should be in front of your knees.

4) Lower and stick out your bottom. This will straighten your back.

5) Try to squeeze your shoulderblades together to push out your chest.

6) Keep your eyes on your target.

It is important to regularly practise forming the scrum with your teammates. Establish a routine and stick to it – your team is counting on you!

OUT NOW